Chicago
Bound

May each day
be an adventure

G Vogl

Praise for *Chicago Bound: A Jake McGreevy Novel (Book Two)*

☆☆☆☆☆ "Art, mystery, music, humor, and adventure— *Chicago Bound* has it all. . . . This is a grand read."

—*Jack Magnus, Readers' Favorite*

"*Chicago Bound* is a powerful new Jake McGreevy novel for middle-grade audiences. . . . Readers will be fascinated to the end."

—*Diane Donovan, Senior eBook Reviewer, Midwest Book Review*

"Having spent many years searching for Mary Cassatt's 1893 mural done for Chicago's World's Fair, I was delighted to encounter Sean Vogel's *Chicago Bound*. . . . [A] thrill-packed adventure. . . . [it] is loving and eventful, and most of all a great read."

—*Sally Webster, author of* Eve's Daughter: Modern Woman, a Mural by Mary Cassatt

Praise for *Celtic Run: A Jake McGreevy Novel (Book One)*

"Romance, danger, intrigue, and personality clashes between peers . . . all make *Celtic Run* a vivid coming-of-age novel."

—*Diane Donovan, eBook Reviewer, Midwest Book Review*

☆☆☆☆☆ "*Celtic Run* is a fast-paced, action-filled novel. . . . The action starts within the first couple of pages and doesn't stop, as cars are hotwired, cliffs are dived off of, and fears are conquered." —*Kayti Nika Raet, Readers' Favorite*

Awards for *Celtic Run: A Jake McGreevy Novel*
IBPA's Benjamin Franklin Awards:
A Silver Medal Winner (Young Reader: Fiction)

The Mom's Choice Awards:
A Gold Recipient (Juvenile Books)

Dan Poynter's Global eBook Awards:
Winner (Children's Literature)

A Jake McGreevy Novel

Chicago Bound

SEAN VOGEL

MB PUBLISHING

ISBNs:
Softcover: 978-0-9850814-5-4
Epub: 978-0-9850814-6-1
Kindle: 978-0-9850814-7-8
Library of Congress Control Number: 2013943391

Paintings by J Loren Reedy, www.jlorenreedy.com
Cover: *A River Runs Through It (2)*; Opening: *Chicago Twilight*;
Closing: *Chicago Art Institute*

Photo Credits
Cover background © istockphoto.com/hudiemm; Chapter 1: Teddy bear
© istockphoto.com/Picsfive; Chapter 2: Pizza slice © istockphoto.com/vikif;
Chapter 3: Latke © istockphoto.com/AnajaCreatif; Chapter 4: Umbrella
© istockphoto.com/alexandre17; Chapter 5: Velvet rope © istockphoto.com/
GlobalStock; Chapter 6: Leather diary © istockphoto.com/brookebecker;
Chapter 7: Backpack © istockphoto.com/Amorphis; Chapter 8: Butterfly
© istockphoto.com/AmbientIdeas; Chapter 9: Violin © istockphoto.com/J-Elgaard;
Chapter 10: Paintbrushes © istockphoto.com/ajma_pl; Chapter 11: Tulips
© istockphoto.com/Acik; Chapter 12: Cup of cocoa © istockphoto.com/bmcent1;
Chapter 13: Knitting © istockphoto.com/TarpMagnus; Chapter 14: Ribbon
© istockphoto.com/Bombaert; Chapter 15: Multitool © istockphoto.com/bluefox42;
Chapter 16: Badge © istockphoto.com/rappensuncle; Chapter 17: Microphone
© istockphoto.com/kenneth-cheung; Chapter 18: Nickels © istockphoto.com/
eldadcarin; Chapter 19: Gift box © istockphoto.com/serdar415; Chapter 20:
Yuletide log © istockphoto.com/redmal; Chapter 21: Apple © istockphoto.com/
Cameramannz; Chapter 22: Frame © istockphoto.com/Crisma; Chapter 23:
Architectural plan © istockphoto.com/chromatika; Chapter 24: Fire alarm pull
© istockphoto.com/sidewaysdesign; Chapter 25: Music stand © istockphoto.com/
marioiram; Chapter 26: Barometer © istockphoto.com/Paul Maguire; Chapter 27:
Books © istockphoto.com/iSebastian; Chapter 28: Walnuts © istockphoto.com/
eyewave; Chapter 29: Mirror © istockphoto.com/Adam Radosavljevic; Chapter
30: Thermos © istockphoto.com/_human; Chapter 31: Bow © istockphoto.com/
adisa; Chapter 32: Magnets © istockphoto.com/stocknshares; Chapter 33: Baking
ingredients © istockphoto.com/shawn_hempel; Chapter 34: Hand weights
© istockphoto.com/AsherDB; Chapter 35: Menorah © istockphoto.com/
BrAt_PiKaChU; Epilogue: Fountain pen © istockphoto.com/JoseIgnacioSoto

Page 51: Reprinted, by permission, from Stanley Appelbaum, *Spectacle in the White
City: The Chicago 1893 World's Fair*, p. 83, ©2009 by Calla Editions, an imprint
of Dover Publications, Inc.; **Page 125:** Reprinted, by permission, from Stanley
Appelbaum, *Spectacle in the White City: The Chicago 1893 World's Fair*, p. 81, ©2009
by Calla Editions, an imprint of Dover Publications, Inc.; **Page 173:** Reprinted, by
permission, from Stanley Appelbaum, *Spectacle in the White City: The Chicago 1893
World's Fair*, p. 8, ©2009 by Calla Editions, an imprint of Dover Publications, Inc.;
Pages 174 and 175: Reprinted, by permission, from Stanley Appelbaum, *Spectacle
in the White City: The Chicago 1893 World's Fair*, p. 82, ©2009 by Calla Editions, an
imprint of Dover Publications, Inc.

For my daughter, Emma,
whose smile melts my heart
and whose laugh sings to my soul.

Chapter 1

Sunday Afternoon (December 21st)

Jake inspected the figure-eight knot that secured his harness to the climbing rope. He watched the slack tighten until he felt a slight upward tug and then reached back to grab a pinch of chalk. Rubbing his palms together, he prepared to make his first move onto the indoor rock wall.

"Climbing!" Jake shouted with a little more gusto than needed, given that his partner, Ben, was only a few feet away.

"Climb on," Ben replied as he worked the ropes through his belaying device.

The rock-climbing gym was conveniently located near Jake's home in Manhattan, but it was also insanely crowded. Consuming nearly a city block, the gym boasted the most diverse selection of routes of all the indoor fitness centers in the tri-state area. Membership was also wildly expensive, but Jake had splurged on it with some of his own money. Last summer, he'd had a fantastic and dangerous adventure in Ireland, culminating in the discovery of some long-hidden treasure, and once he'd returned home, he had zealously embarked on an exercise program, having come to the conclusion that it was important to be prepared for *anything*.

The beginner's bouldering area was behind them near the entrance. And the gym's most complex routes, with the most challenging holds, were farther down the line. To gain access to those routes, Jake and Ben would have to prove themselves on this 5.6 Yosemite Decimal System–rated climb. Attempting to tune out the masses of people around him, Jake placed his foot on the first climbing hold and hoisted himself onto the wall. His toes screamed in pain. *Rats. Forgot to cut my toenails again.* By design, rock shoes are extremely tight, and the millimeter of extra length his nails added quadrupled the pain factor.

With purpose and care, Jake made move after move until he was nearly forty feet in the air. He shook his head to flip his shaggier-than-normal sandy blond hair from his eyes. As best he could tell, the next handhold was a good eighteen inches higher than his reach. Although he'd hit a growth spurt over the summer, Jake was still well below average height for a fifteen-year-old. He looked down at Ben. "I'm not sure about this next move."

Ben nodded and pulled any remaining slack out of the rope so that if Jake missed the hold, he wouldn't fall too far. Tall and slim, with a mop of red curly hair, Ben had become a good friend of Jake's. He occupied second-chair violin—right next to Jake, in first chair—in the school's orchestra. They were both freshman at a large private New York City high school, and together they'd weathered the difficult middle-to-high-school transition. Knowing that later tonight they would be cramped inside a bus heading to a performing arts camp in Chicago, where they'd spend winter break, Jake and Ben were grateful to squeeze in some physical exercise before heading west.

Lunging, Jake stretched for the climbing hold. His fingers curled around the tiny grip and his muscles strained as his entire weight was suspended in the air, supported only by his right hand. He flexed and lifted himself up by one arm, just enough to get his other hand onto a hold. Moments later, he'd found decent footholds and took a minute to catch his breath.

"Nice move," Ben called from below.

"Thanks!" Jake smiled down at him. *Good thing I added pull-ups to my workout routine.*

CRACK! The sound of metal cracking echoed throughout the facility, followed quickly by a scream. Jake swiveled his head in the direction of the noise. On the route next to his, a middle-aged woman swung suspended in the air. Jake tilted his head to examine the pulley system that was attached to the top of the rock wall. It had separated from its mount and appeared as if it could give way at any time. "Ben!" Jake called.

"Go, Jake, go!"

From the moment they'd met, Jake and Ben had instantly been on the same wavelength. Whether it was music, climbing, movies, or girls, they always seemed to know what was on the other's mind. Jake let go of the rock holds and let the rope take his weight, snapping him into a position that was perpendicular to the wall. He ran sideways along the fake rock like a Cirque du Soleil acrobat as Ben expertly played out the slack. There was another loud snap, and Jake dove and wrapped his arms around the woman. She screamed as the pulley system gave way. Jake grunted as her entire weight bore down on him. Like a pendulum, Jake and the woman swung back toward his part of the rock wall. Ben let the rope slide freely and the two of them glided quickly but softly to the ground.

Immediately, the woman's climbing partner and the facility's staff descended upon them.

"You . . . you saved my life." The woman was near tears.

"Well, it was teamwork." Jake stood up and brushed himself off. He went to high-five Ben but stopped when he saw blood dripping from his friend's fingers. "Wicked rope burn!"

"I wanted to make sure you two descended fast in case it was difficult to hold onto her," Ben said, wiping the blood onto his shorts.

"Good call, Ben. Hope it doesn't interfere with your violin playing, though." Jake took a step backward from the crowd of people enveloping them.

*   *   *

By the time Jake made it home to the two-story brownstone he shared with his father, the cell phone video of the rescue had garnered thousands of hits.

"Quick thinking, son," Mr. McGreevy said, greeting Jake as he walked through the door. "There are more than a few messages by the phone from reporters wanting to talk with you."

"No thanks," Jake said, as he shed his shoes by the front door and followed his dad into the kitchen. "After last summer, I think I've had enough of reporters. Besides, Ben and I were just at the right place at the right time—that's all."

"I understand, Jake," his dad said, giving his son a quick pat.

Their townhouse was very similar to the other hundred or so in the neighborhood—with the exception of the widened doorways and the mini-elevator that went to the second floor. Mr. McGreevy had been paralyzed after a horse-riding accident nearly two years before, and their house had been modified to accommodate his wheelchair.

"Dinner smells good. What is it?" Jake bent down to peer into the oven.

"Osso buco with a savory rosemary-balsamic reduction," Mr. McGreevy replied.

"I assumed it was pizza," Jake said.

"Of course it's pizza." Mr. McGreevy smiled and Jake laughed, their running joke continuing for another night. Mr. McGreevy, despite his exacting architect's mind, disliked following recipes and cooking, so they tended to eat a lot of pizza.

"It won't be ready for a few more minutes. Remember our deal? You have to finish unpacking that last box before you leave tonight for Chicago," he said as he rolled over to the cupboard to get some silverware.

"All right," Jake grumbled, heading upstairs to his room. They'd moved into their brownstone two months ago, but Jake hadn't yet finished going through the last box. He entered his room and padded over to it. Lifting the lid, he stared at the old things strewn about. *What am I going to do with all this junk?* He shuffled through the matchbox cars, empty CD jewel cases, and pieces of electronic gear that even he, with his knack for fixing things, couldn't save. He spotted a medium-sized teddy bear. "The Art Institute of Chicago" read the bear's shirt. Chicago: Jake hadn't really thought about it before, but he suddenly realized that he was going to the same city where his mother had died.

He freed the stuffed animal from its cardboard dwelling and sat on the bed with it. *My mom bought this for me, right before . . .* Two years old then, Jake couldn't remember receiving the gift, but he did recall his dad telling him when he was young that it was the last gift his mother had purchased. *Dad was so angry when he found me roughhousing with the bear.* After that incident, Jake had let the bear sit on a shelf in the closet. He gazed into the bear's eyes. *Who was she?* Lately, his father had opened up a little more and discussed the mother he never knew, but he still felt a persistent emptiness.

Turning the bear over, he saw some brown thread, slightly off color from the rest of the stitching along the seam. *Never noticed that before.* The string was loose and Jake gently tugged on it. The bottom of the bear separated, revealing a yellowed piece of folded paper.

Dear Richard,

*I'm sorry you couldn't be here to explore the city with me.
I took a break to clear my head and went to the Chicago
Theatre. You simply must read the notes in my binder so
you can understand what I experienced. The Art Deco
sconces on the second floor remind me of our spectacular
time in Paris together.*

Love,

Karen

The date at the top nearly leapt off the page. *The day she
was killed! She died outside the theater, so she must have written
this note just moments before. What's it doing inside my bear?*

Chapter 2

Sunday Evening (December 21st)

"Jake, dinner!" Mr. McGreevy's voice echoed from downstairs. Jake stuffed the note back into the bear and placed it inside his backpack. Slowly making his way downstairs, he tried to compose himself so as not to give away the confusion roiling his mind. He entered the kitchen, grabbed a drink from the refrigerator, and plopped down at the table.

"Did you unpack the box?" Mr. McGreevy asked.

"Just about. I'm not sure what to do with it all. It's mostly stuff that I should throw away," Jake replied as he picked up a slice of pizza. He chewed without interest, the flavor lost on him.

"Looks like that pizza is eating you more than you're eating it," his father said.

"Hmm?"

"I said, what's on your mind, son?"

I need a better poker face. "Sorry. I was just thinking that I was going to Chicago, and . . . well, that's where Mom died."

Mr. McGreevy stared at his son, his eyes almost misty. "I've thought about that every day since you showed me the flyer about the performing arts camp."

"I don't have to go," Jake responded.

"No, you *should* go. The chance to learn from the best and experience new things is too good to pass up. I know nothing bad will happen, but it's a father's prerogative to worry about his son who's going away for two weeks."

Especially to the city where your wife died, Jake finished his dad's thought. "What was she doing there?" Jake hated to push his father, knowing the pain of her death was still great, but he needed to know.

"You are so much like her, it's amazing. When I learned you found that Spanish treasure last summer, I thought, 'He's just like Karen.' You see, your mom was always trying to solve historical mysteries. She was a wonderful artist, but her real talent was verifying provenance."

"What's provenance?" Jake asked.

"It's the backstory, or origin, of an artifact. For example, let's say you have a baseball signed by Mickey Mantle that your grandfather gave to you. It might do well at auction. But if you have a signed baseball *and* a picture of your grandfather standing with Mickey Mantle, then the value increases because you can *prove* provenance."

"Because you can clearly show it's a genuine signature?" Jake said.

"Exactly."

"So Mom was like a history detective?" Jake asked, referring to his dad's favorite TV show.

"That's a good way of putting it. Not only did she have the determination to follow trails and pursue leads, but she had a strong eye for artistic style and detail. I see that same analytical and tenacious mind in you, Jake."

Jake felt his cheeks get red. His dad was great at building up his confidence, but it never failed to embarrass him, even though nobody else was in the kitchen to hear the compliment.

"So she went to Chicago to investigate something?"

"Not just *something*. A huge sixty-four-foot painting by the famous American Impressionist Mary Cassatt, which had been missing for more than a hundred years. The Art Institute contacted your mom and asked her to come to Chicago to validate it before they purchased it. She had already made quite a name for herself in the art world as one of the most thorough researchers in her field, but this assignment was going to be her biggest yet. And although she enjoyed her investigative work, her dream was to land a permanent position with a museum in New York City, so really, this opportunity would have helped her . . ." Mr. McGreevy's voice trailed off.

Jake drained the last of his iced tea. His gut twisted as he tried to decide if he should tell his father about what he had just found inside the bear. *No, he's already struggling with my going to Chicago. It can wait for now.*

*   *   *

After dinner, Jake scurried up to his room to finish packing. He and Ben, along with Jake's lifelong friend Julie, were part of a select group headed to Chicago for a performing arts camp called Sound in Motion. Combining musicians from high school orchestras with rhythmic gymnasts, the camp offered daily mentorship from the top performers in their fields. The winter break program paired holiday music with the athletic but dancelike rhythmic gymnastics. The camp would be holding several concerts to raise money for music programs in underserved schools across the country that had been hit hard by the economy and Mother Nature. Jake and Ben were representing their school's orchestra. Julie had managed to gain the last place on the gymnastics roster when she narrowly beat her chief rival in a head-to-head competition. At first, Jake was thrilled to be spending this time with his friends, but the stress of having to perform on stage with the best of the best, combined with the regret that his father would be alone for the holidays, made him wonder if he should be going.

Jake had filled his suitcase with the usual items, like clothes and toiletries, and his violin and accessories were packed and waiting by the door. But he had yet to select which gadgets to bring. He worked part-time at a security and spy shop, which gave him access to tons of cool gizmos. *Two weeks in Chicago, crammed into an old school building with a hundred other students. What could I possibly need? Maybe I'll just keep it simple.* He spotted his fiber-optic camera sitting on a shelf and smiled at the memory of its use in Ireland. *Camera—check.* He also packed the essentials required by any gadget whiz: a Leatherman multi-tool, Maglite LED flashlight, and duct tape.

Satisfied, Jake zipped up his backpack and set it next to his luggage.

"Jake, the taxi is here to take you to the bus," Mr. McGreevy called.

Jake grabbed his things and hustled down the stairs. "Wish we were flying instead of driving."

"I can see the wisdom in taking a bus at night. It's cheaper than airfare—and by driving all night, they're hoping the kids will sleep instead of getting rowdy." Mr. McGreevy stretched up from his chair to tussle Jake's hair.

"Hey, Dad?" Jake paused in the doorway.

Jake's dad stopped and spun his wheelchair on the hardwood floor.

"Yes?"

"I saw an advertisement for a school trip this spring from the civics department. Kids from around the world are going to spend ten days setting up a mock government and such."

"You haven't even gone on this trip yet. You keep running away like this and I'll get a complex!" Mr. McGreevy winked at him.

"Maybe I just want to eat something other than pizza," Jake laughed.

Mr. McGreevy fake snarled at him. "Where's this one—the moon?"

"Closer. Paris."

"We'll talk about it when you return. I'm not so sure about another overseas excursion . . . although Paris does sound good. Your mom and I often talked about going but we never made the trip." Mr. McGreevy hugged his son goodbye.

Jake stopped halfway to the taxi and turned to see his dad waving. He was so excited about the possibility of actually going to Paris that it took a moment for his dad's answer to sink in.

He's never been to Paris? But the note in the bear said "our time in Paris together." Dad couldn't have forgotten about a trip to Paris . . . My mom was trying to tell him something!

Chapter 3

Sunday Evening (December 21st)

The noise on the bus was deafening and grew in intensity each time another kid climbed the stairs. Jake and Ben sat next to each other about halfway down the aisle.

"Latke? I tried a new recipe that says you can serve them cold." Ben unzipped a plastic bag and offered a traditional potato pancake to Jake.

"Definitely!" Jake pulled a treat from the bag. "Tomorrow's the first night of Hanukkah, right? What are you going to do about the candles?"

"I guess you've rubbed off on me, as I now cart around gadgets just in case." Ben brandished a miniature battery-operated menorah from his backpack. "They're LED, so it should easily last all season."

Jake chuckled. "It'll be a little ironic if the batteries die before the eighth day, seeing how the story is about the long-burning oil."

Ben smiled. "Yes, that *would* be bad. Hey, I know Christmas is still a few days away, but did you and your dad open your gifts before you left?"

"No. Even though we'll be here through Christmas and New Year's, it wasn't a big deal to wait. I'm fifteen. It's not like I'm rushing down the stairs early in the morning to see what Santa's brought," Jake replied.

Jake's best friend, Julie, boarded the bus and sat in an

open seat across from them. She was nearly 5'8", which made her the tallest gymnast on her team. For the longest time, Jake had yearned to be her boyfriend. But since last summer, his feelings had mellowed somewhat.

Sharing her seat was a petite girl with wavy shoulder-length chestnut hair and a heart-shaped face. She had a youthful appearance, but Jake had caught how her keen eyes sized up each person stepping onto the bus. *I bet there's a lot going on behind that cute face.*

"Hi, I'm Jake McGreevy. I play the violin." Jake extended his arm past Julie to shake the girl's hand.

"Natalie Silver, also violin," she said.

"I know that name. You're first chair over at East High," Jake said.

"East just has a small orchestra, though." She smiled shyly.

But you're probably the best musician on the bus. "These are my friends, Julie O'Brien and Ben Meyers." Jake elbowed Ben, who was absorbed in his tablet PC.

Natalie brightened. "Hi, Julie, Ben! Hmm, Ben Meyers. Are you related to Danny Meyers?"

"Yes, he's my brother," Ben uttered with all the enthusiasm of a dental patient waiting for his root canal procedure to get underway.

"I saw him at Carnegie Hall last year. He's an amazing pianist. Do you play the piano, too?" Natalie asked.

"No, I torture the violin." Ben's joke generated a look of confusion on Natalie's face.

Free of city traffic, the bus accelerated onto the highway and most of the kids settled down, either to sleep or concentrate on their electronic devices. Jake pulled a Chicago tour book from his backpack.

"You want to use my digital version? It has pictures and videos." Ben offered his computer to Jake.

"No, thanks. I enjoy guidebooks. I like to bend the pages of the places I want to see." Jake switched on the light above his seat but the bulb didn't turn on.

"I already tried them. They don't work. Another reason to progress from the Stone Age: backlit screen." Ben thumped the LCD on his computer.

Jake stared up at the ceiling. The light assembly was housed beneath a shelf for small luggage. The shelf had a narrow railing to prevent objects from sliding off and striking passengers. Jake bent over and pulled a shoestring out of his running shoe and then retrieved his Maglite flashlight from his backpack. Using a clove hitch knot, he lashed the light to the railing and adjusted the beam to shine directly onto his seat.

As he sat down again, he caught Natalie's eye. *She's staring at me.*

"Is that the Maglite XL200?" she asked.

Jake's heart pounded. "Uh, yes. Good eye."

"I have the XL*100*." She smiled before returning to her magazine.

Never knew a girl to recognize gear like that before. Jake turned around to see if Ben had heard the exchange, but he was concentrating on his video game. Jake retrieved the foldout map from the Chicago guide and studied it intently.

"What are you looking for?" Julie leaned over the aisle.

"The intersection where my mother died," Jake responded. "A hit-and-run driver struck her at the corner of East Benton Place and North State Street, right by the Chicago Theatre. They never caught the guy," Jake said.

"My goodness." Natalie put her hand to her heart.

"We should visit where she died. I can say Kaddish, the mourner's prayer," Ben said.

Although Jake and his dad weren't all that religious, they

had respect for spirituality and tradition, and Jake knew that Judaism was important to Ben's family. "I'd really like that. Thanks, Ben."

* * *

The drama at the rock climbing gym, the mysterious note from his mother, and the overall anxiety about the performing arts camp kept sleep at bay. Just when Jake didn't think he could take the confinement of the bus anymore, they turned north off Interstate 80 and headed into a cold Chicago morning. The low clouds and the fog hadn't yet burned off, and a dull gray sky dashed any hopes of their seeing the Willis Tower or the John Hancock Center. Chatter and excitement intensified and Jake started packing away all his gear, with the exception of the foldout map.

"Are we there yet?" Ben yawned as he stretched himself awake.

"Not quite, but we're approaching the south branch of the Chicago River, so Stanley House can't be too far away."

"Found it." Ben peered at his tablet, which was connected to the Internet through his cell phone hotspot. "Looks like this boarding school is smack in the middle of a residential area, but overall, it's not far from the big attractions, like Shedd Aquarium and the Field Museum."

For the next twenty minutes, the bus carved its way through the southern and mostly industrial part of Chicago. Eventually, it turned off the road onto a tree-lined driveway. Emerging from the mini-forest, it rolled to a stop before a massive iron gate in front of the century-old boarding school, which would be, for the next two weeks anyway, the kids' performing arts camp. The driver spoke to the guard, who, after checking his clipboard, waved the bus in.

"This doesn't look as inviting in person as it does in the brochure," Julie said as she peered out the window.

20

"I'll say. It's more prison than school," Ben commented.

"What?" Jake said. "You guys just don't know how to appreciate architecture! Look—it's great. The wall we just passed is pure Chicago brick—the original type. That kind of brick is a collector's item, and you'd never be able to afford to build a fence using brick like that today." Thanks to his architect father, Jake had little interest in baseball cards or sports cars, but he had an outsized appreciation for construction and design.

"Jake's right. Old Chicago brick is about $2.24 per square foot versus 30 cents a square foot for standard brick," Ben read from his computer.

"I smell a challenge: brain versus computer!" Julie's eyes sparkled in the dim light. "We're approaching the building. Whoever can describe the architecture faster wins—Jake the brainiac or Ben the computer whiz."

Jake looked over at Ben who returned his nod. "Contest!" they replied, bumping fists.

"Go!" Julie said. "*Buona fortuna,*" she added, happily sprinkling in some Italian she'd learned in school last semester.

Jake studied the massive structure and tried to block out the furious typing coming from Ben. "English bond brickwork, recessed and arched entranceways, elongated water spouts—"

"Stanley House boasts rustication on the corners, tracery or shapes creating a pattern in the windows." Ben's reading interrupted Jake's description.

"Collegiate Gothic!" the boys yelled in unison.

"Tie," Julie called, as nearby students shot them weird looks.

"So we both win?" Jake asked.

"Nope. A draw isn't a W."

"What was the prize, anyway?" Ben asked.

Julie leaned across the aisle close to Jake and Ben, her

light-scented perfume invading their noses. "It would have been a kiss," she winked.

Jake, who was used to some of the flirtatious things Julie said, knew she was kidding, but Ben withdrew back into his seat. *Poor Ben. He's not great with girls.* Julie was one of the friendliest and best-looking girls in the school—not conceited in any way, and tomboyish enough to be fun to hang out with—and she had many suitors. Jake wouldn't have been surprised if Ben was one of the hopefuls.

The kids retrieved their luggage from under the bus and were ushered up the steps and into the building by a young man wearing an apple-red parka with "Stanley House" emblazoned on the front. "Okay, line up, kids, in three rows of twelve students each!"

It took several noisy minutes for everyone to arrange themselves into even rows. The reception area was a cavernous room with granite floors and dark wood paneling. Several tapestries and paintings hung on the walls, the faces in them glowering at the students. Holiday decorations added the only warmth to the room. A large switchback staircase led to additional floors, and Jake found his pulse increase. *Can't wait to explore this old building.*

BANG!

Chapter 4

Monday Morning (December 22nd)

A sharp sound of metal striking the hard stone floor echoed throughout the hall, and the kids stopped talking.

"Much too slow. In the future, when you're told to line up, you will do so, quietly, in less than thirty seconds." A tall reedy man with bushy eyebrows and a creased face walked to the front of the group. A poor dye job left his hair too dark, with a few streaks of silver filtering through. He was carrying a large umbrella with a metal tip and with each step, like a cane, the tip hit the floor.

"I'm the dean of the school. You may call me Dean Stanley. My great-grandfather founded this facility and it's been run by a Stanley ever since." The man paced back and forth.

"You're here because you're talented. Shortly, another thirty students will join you. Although volunteer professionals from each area of expertise will be instructing you, I'm responsible for your well-being. When school is in session, we are home to elite students from around the world. The rooms and the amenities are all exceptional, and I want you to keep them in the same pristine condition in which you will find them. To reach your level of achievement took focus and discipline, and I expect you to apply that same control to your behavior *outside* the music room or gymnasium, as well."

"Ben was right. This *is* prison," Julie whispered from the side of her mouth.

"One demerit for Ms. O'Brien," Dean Stanley bellowed as he marched right up to Julie.

"That's right. I know who you are." He spun around to the rest of the group. "I know who all of you are. We work on the demerit system here. Amass five demerits and you'll find yourself back home. Let me give you some advice. Focus and discipline are the foundations of success. So focus now on the rules and be disciplined each day and I can almost guarantee that you'll be successful here. You might even *enjoy* yourselves. Now, without further ado, here's the schedule: You must line up like so each morning at six in the gymnasium." A groan emerged from the kids. "Breakfast is served from 6:05 to 7:00. You will be in class until 11:00. Lunch will commence at 11:45. At 3:00 P.M., you will have two hours for private study or one-on-one training with your coaches or instructors. The rest of the time will be yours—to use wisely, I'm sure. You will gather in the gymnasium at a quarter past five for evening roll call and then have dinner, which ends precisely at 6:30. After that, it is more study time or private training sessions or, on certain days, evening performances at various venues in the city. Lights out, and I mean lights *out*, is at 10:00 P.M. Any questions?"

Jake glanced around. Most of the kids were too fearful to raise their hands. *I have one: Are you practicing for the role of Scrooge in this year's* A Christmas Carol?

"Ah, one more thing. For those of you who didn't notice, we have state-of-the-art security here, designed to keep you safe from the outside. However, we can only keep you safe if you're here, so any attempt to leave the grounds without permission will result in immediate expulsion from the program. Now, line up for your room assignments." The Dean motioned to the uniformed staff waiting patiently nearby. Jake and Ben lucked out and ended up rooming together. The floors were segregated, with the boys on the third floor and the girls on the second floor.

"We're in room 305. Where are you, Julie?" Jake asked as the three of them dragged their luggage up the switchback stairs.

"I have my own room—207," Julie grumbled.

"That's great. Wonder how that happened," Ben said.

"Guess," Julie responded.

"Your dad pulled strings?" Jake said.

"*Giusto*. As usual, my dad means well, but I'd rather just be a regular student, not the rich girl." Julie stopped at the entrance to the second-floor hallway. "This is me."

"It's only ten o'clock and the first activity on the agenda doesn't start until three. I was hoping we could go inside the Chicago Theatre, but since we're confined to this building, I don't know what we're going to do."

"Inside? I thought you just wanted to visit the intersection," Julie said.

Jake told her and Ben about the note he'd found hidden inside the bear and the fact that his parents had never been to Paris.

"Okay, but I still don't see what's important about the theater," Ben said.

"Well, I think my mom mentioned Paris to clue my father in that something wasn't right. She went to a lot of trouble to talk about the Art Deco sconces—you know, decorative light fixtures—but I read in my guidebook that the Chicago Theatre was built using French Baroque architecture. Art Deco wouldn't fit . . . the styles are totally different," Jake said.

"Oh, now I get it," Ben said. "But you're right. The Dean made it pretty clear we can't just wander off."

"That's what he said, all right." Jake frowned, furrowing his brow and trying to think his way around this roadblock.

Chapter 5

Monday Morning (December 22nd)

"Wait—I've got it!" Julie said. "We can just ask Dean Stanley to let us go see where your mom was killed. Then, when we're there, we can go inside the theater. I mean, I know it sounds kind of insensitive to use that as an excuse, but what adult could say no . . . ?" Her voice trailed off and she raised her hand to her mouth as if to take back her suggestion.

"It's not insensitive—it's brilliant," Jake responded. "And anyway, it's the truth."

Jake approached the Dean, who, although not thrilled with the idea, was unable to say no, just as Julie had predicted. He ordered a staff member to drive them to the intersection by the Chicago Theatre. Julie had spotted Natalie in the hallway and invited her along. The four kids piled into a 15-passenger van. The driver pointed out famous landmarks along the way. When they arrived, he pulled to the curb to let them out.

"I think we need about thirty minutes. Is that okay?" Jake asked the driver as he hopped out of the van.

"Sure. I've got a quick errand I can do in the meantime."

The marquee advertised that Charles Dickens's *A Christmas Carol* was currently running, and the famous Chicago Theatre sign was aglow in red lights. Jake ignored the entranceway and stared at the street. Cars whizzed by at alarming speeds. *My mom didn't stand a chance.* Jake fought a losing battle against a tear. He felt Julie move closer to him and reached to hold her hand.

"The police report said that the driver was heading north at 40 miles per hour," Jake said. "There weren't any skid marks, but they did find the car a few days later: a stolen work van that smelled of alcohol."

"Drunk driving—perhaps the most selfish crime," Ben muttered.

"That was the theory. Case went cold pretty quickly," said Jake, his voice cracking.

They all held hands and Ben recited a few prayers. Natalie, also knowing the words of the Kaddish, joined in with Ben. When they finished, they remained silent. Jake blocked out the loud noise of the cars. Although he couldn't remember his mother, he always felt a connection to her. Maybe it was the memory of her smell or her touch that reached him subconsciously. On special occasions—like birthdays, the first day of school, holidays—and sometimes, when he glimpsed something as simple as a hug between a mother and her child—Jake sensed the hole in his heart growing larger, a yearning to know her that could never be fulfilled. The pictures he'd seen of her flashed through his mind. *Why did she have to die?*

When they were finished, Jake led them into the building. With hours to go until show time, the theater was nevertheless open to tourists and other people interested in purchasing tickets. The lobby was striking, just as the guidebook had promised: reaching five stories to a domed tiled ceiling, the plush red space was as ornate as it was bold.

"Wow. I hope I get to play *here* one day!" Natalie exclaimed. "Look at that staircase: it reminds me of the one I saw in the Paris Opera House last summer."

Jake's heart skipped a beat. "That's right! I read in the guidebook that this staircase was modeled after the one in Paris."

"And just look at that chandelier." Natalie continued to gaze at the extraordinary space.

"My mom's note mentioned sconces on the second floor," Jake said, heading toward the grand staircase. "Uh-oh. Roadblock." A thick velvet rope stood in their way.

"Guess they don't want people to go upstairs," Ben said.

Ugh! Why is nothing easy? Jake swiveled his head, searching for anyone who might be watching them.

"I know that face. That's your determined look," Julie said.

"I've known Jake for only a few months and I've learned he doesn't accept simple obstacles like a rope across the stairs," Ben muttered.

"*Ah, sicuramente!*" Julie said. "You can say that again!" Julie knew that her Italian wouldn't always be understood, so she'd developed the habit of translating sentences into English.

"He's got chutzpah, that's for sure!" Ben added, smiling.

Jake snickered and ducked under the rope. Ben and Julie, both tall for their age, had no issues in hurdling it. Natalie gracefully unclipped the rope, stepped through, and then reattached it.

Jake, Ben, and Julie crouched low and hugged the railing, trying to avoid anyone seeing them scuttling up the stairs. Jake glanced over and saw Natalie walking up the middle of the majestic stairway, holding onto the center banister. "What are you *doing?*" he whispered.

"I'm afraid of heights. Even just walking near the edge of the stairs makes me dizzy," she replied.

Oy. "Well, just try to keep a low profile," Jake said.

"Will do," Natalie whispered.

As quietly as they could, they hustled to the top. Mercifully, the second floor was deserted.

"OK, let's check out all the fixtures and see if one sticks out as odd," Jake murmured as he sprinted to the nearest one. Spreading out, the kids inspected each wall sconce, even wiggling them to see if they were firmly attached.

"Over here!" Ben called.

Jake cringed, hoping the staff downstairs didn't hear him.

"Look—the initials KM are etched on the side." Ben pointed to tiny letters on the sconce.

"Karen McGreevy. That has to be it." Jake yanked his well-used Leatherman tool from his backpack. In a matter of seconds, he had the screws out. Ben pivoted the bronze fixture on the remaining screw. Tiny fragments of plaster fell to the ground from the hole in the wall behind the light. Jake pushed the electrical wires protruding from the hole to the side. Reaching inside, he searched with his fingers.

"There's something in here!" Jake retracted his hand, pulling out a thick notebook. The others huddled around Jake as he opened it. "It's my mother's handwriting." Jake stumbled on the words, a river of emotions flooding his mind.

"I don't understand. Why would she hide it in here?" Julie asked.

"I don't know, but we'd better get out of here and talk about it later." Jake helped Ben remount the light and then hurried down the stairs. Detained by a theater worker, they received a brief and half-hearted scolding for being upstairs. Happy to have avoided a big scene, the gang flagged down the Stanley House driver.

Out of view of the driver, Jake opened the notebook. The pages were brittle and slightly yellow. Some text, hastily written on the inside cover, stung him.

Sweet Richard,

If you're reading this, something terrible has happened.

Chapter 6

Monday Afternoon (December 22nd)

The kids returned to Stanley House just in time to have a quick lunch. Jake couldn't wait to read his mother's notes, but the aroma of delicious food overwhelmed him. He gawked at the robust selection in the dining hall. *This is definitely not typical school food.* Organized in a large oval, the stations consisted of salads, pastas, pizzas, grilled selections, vegetables, fruits, and sandwiches. The sign on the international station read, "Today's Featured Flavor Is Moroccan."

"Well, it's official!" Julie said, mouth agape. "I'm going to gain about twenty pounds."

"I bet you won't. They'll keep you so active that you'll probably need every extra calorie you can get," Jake responded.

"Hey, Jake, check this out," Ben called from an island in the center of the oval. Next to a beverage dispenser was a huge cooler full of different flavors of ice cream, gelato, and frozen yogurt.

"Score!" Jake bounded over to review the display. "I wonder how long I can survive on just ice cream."

The others laughed and peeled off quickly with plates in hand. Jake scanned the selections again. *I'm actually craving pizza. Maybe I'm thinking about home too much.*

Jake grabbed a slice, a drink, and a scoop of rocky road before catching up to the others, who were sitting in the far corner of the room.

"They weren't kidding when they said the meals were

fantastic," Ben remarked as he dug into a bowl of spaghetti and vegetable-filled tomato sauce. "Bon appétit!"

"*Buon appetito,*" Julie responded. "You *are* eating *spaghetti,* right, Ben?"

"Roger that." Ben smiled.

"Well, whatta ya know. If it isn't Daddy Warbucks's little girl." A snooty voice pierced the chaos.

Jake swiveled his head. *Oh, no.* Samantha Rigby, Julie's chief rival and nemesis, strolled toward their table, followed by her two look-alike minions. Samantha was petite, with short blonde hair, and wore expensive jeans and a custom-tailored faux fur coat.

Jake glanced over at Julie. Her jaw was clenched, and Jake could see the struggle in her eyes. *She's trying to ignore it. Well, I won't.* "I heard one of the other gymnast's broke her ankle and the team needed a sub. I guess they had to scrape the bottom of the barrel." Jake stared at Samantha.

"Well, isn't that romantic. Pint-sized Ken is trying to stand up for his gargantuan Barbie." Samantha's biting comment garnered a chorus of laughter from the students nearby. Julie's face turned red and she mouthed "I'm sorry" to Jake. But Jake hadn't taken his eyes off Samantha as he watched her take a seat at a nearby table. She promptly started texting.

"What's she sportin'?" Ben asked as he hauled his computer out of his shoulder bag.

"Looks like the new Platinum-G350. Could be difficult—heard they're unhackable," Jake responded.

"Nah. Let me know when she presses "send" on her text." Ben's fingers blurred as he typed on the tablet.

"Now!" Jake whisper-yelled.

Ben pressed a button.

"What?! My phone—all the words are in Chinese or something!" Samantha shrieked.

On the down low, Jake gave Ben a fist bump.

Julie leaned across the table. "Impressive . . ."

Ben and Jake beamed and blushed under Julie's praise.

"But I prefer to fight my battles on the competition floor." Julie's smile vanished.

Ben visibly shrank.

Crud. "Sooo . . . Zach's skiing over winter break, right?" Jake tried to change the subject. Zach was Julie's boyfriend, or at least he was when they weren't broken up. Zach used to torment Jake, but after their summer adventure in Ireland, they'd become friends. Not close friends, but no longer sworn enemies.

"Um-hmm. He's in Colorado with his family." Julie's casual attitude signaled to Jake that they were in yet another of their off-again phases.

"Have you heard from Maggie lately?" Julie asked, referring to the friend they'd made and at whose house Jake had stayed in Ireland.

"Yes, she's really excited about the holidays. She's been so busy at the dance school that she hasn't been back home to Dingle since September. And the Colonel flew back to Ireland last week and said he'd swing by the pub and deliver our gifts for everyone," Jake responded. He smiled as he thought back to the summer that he, Julie, Zach, and Maggie had shared. His great-uncle, a retired Irish Army colonel whom Jake had met in Dingle, had come to New York to live with him and his dad after they returned to the States. Now that Jake's father was making great progress in his rehabilitation, the Colonel was able to return to Ireland.

"So what do your parents do?" Jake asked Natalie, who had been quietly listening to their conversation.

"My dad's a dentist. And my mom volunteers at a couple of places," Natalie responded.

"My dad's an architect," Jake said, with a slight tinge of nerves in his voice.

"I gathered from your competition on the bus," she said, smiling.

Jake felt his cheeks heat up. "What about you? What do you like to do for fun?"

"Oh, normal stuff. I like to play Ping-Pong and do little home-repair projects," Natalie replied.

"Ping-Pong, yes. But home repair? I'm not sure I'd call that normal," Julie teased.

This time Natalie's face turned crimson. "I guess not. But my dad isn't very handy—although, he thinks he is, which causes problems. So my mom and I took some fix-it classes and I guess I got hooked on working with my hands."

"What about *your* family?" Natalie directed her question to Ben.

"They're getting a divorce. I mean, I guess that's not really what you asked. My dad's a software programmer." Ben stumbled on the words. "And my mom's an interior designer."

"Sorry to hear about the divorce. That's tough," Natalie said sympathetically. Then she returned to her food.

Out of the corner of his eye, Jake could see Ben's face crumple with frustration.

"I'm going to head up to our room to do some reading." Jake stood and picked up his tray, depositing it on the way out. Ben followed Jake to their room but immediately went to work on his computer game. Jake settled comfortably on his bed and gingerly opened the notebook, trying to absorb the message on the inside cover:

Sweet Richard,

If you're reading this, something terrible has happened.

It was dated the day of her death.

Chapter 7

Thirteen Years Earlier

"Honey, let's go. You'll miss your flight," Richard McGreevy called.

"Coming," Karen answered. Biting her bottom lip, she walked over to Jake, fast asleep in his toddler bed. Her next-door neighbor had agreed to watch him while they rode to La Guardia International Airport for her early-morning flight to Chicago. Bending over, she gave her son a kiss, tucked him into his quilted comforter, and whispered "sweet dreams, cubby" one last time. When he stirred, she quickly stepped away, knowing that if he woke and called for her, she'd never make the plane.

"Are you sure I should go?" she asked.

"Of course. This is the chance of a lifetime. You've been on the trail of this mural for years." Richard picked up his wife's suitcase and walked to the cab that was waiting by the curb. He stowed the soft-sided maroon luggage into the trunk and climbed into the taxi after her.

"I know. But I could be gone for a few weeks and you'll have to watch Jake alone," Karen countered.

"I've got it all under control. I've finished the Alcott Building renovation, and my next job is in the talking phase, so now is as good a time as any for you to go."

"Okay. But please promise me you won't feed him pizza

every night." Karen inched closer and pecked her husband on the cheek.

*   *   *

During the short plane ride, Karen reviewed the letter the Art Institute of Chicago had sent her.

Dear Ms. McGreevy:

As you are undoubtedly already aware, the Mary Cassatt mural that disappeared fourteen years after the close of the 1893 World's Fair has been recently discovered. The Art Institute is preparing to purchase the mural. As part of our due diligence, we are taking all necessary steps to ensure its authenticity.

We would be honored if you would come to Chicago as our guest to verify the painting's provenance and genuineness.

Please contact us at your earliest convenience to discuss your interest in and availability for this most crucial undertaking.

We look forward to hearing from you soon.

Yours truly,

Conner Royal

Deputy Director, Art Institute of Chicago

Karen put the letter away and looked out the window at the approaching city. She'd been to Chicago on several other occasions but each time could admire the skyline with new eyes. She watched as the barges steered into open docks in the industrial section of the city, and then she set her gaze upon the soaring office buildings. *I should have brought Richard and Jake.* Karen's husband adored Chicago, as it was home to noteworthy architectural landmarks, including houses designed by Frank Lloyd Wright. Karen decided she would ask Richard to bring Jake to Chicago if her assignment lasted more than one week.

Chapter 8

Monday Afternoon (December 22nd)

Jake's watch chirped 2:45 P.M., pulling him away from his mom's binder, which was filled with her notions about the missing Cassatt mural and her various efforts to find it. But before he closed the cover, he read a rare personal thought: *I haven't even landed in Chicago yet, and I already miss my guys— my life, my heart, my two sweet loves.*

A lump formed in Jake's throat. *She really loved us.* After wiping his face to ensure there weren't any tears, he tucked her notebook into his backpack and kicked the back of Ben's chair.

"Time already?" Ben asked as he pulled off his headphones.

"Yes. You get too absorbed in that game." Jake picked up his violin.

"I know. But escaping to a different world, one I can actually control, is addictive."

"Where do you stand today?" Jake asked.

"I'm still a hundred points behind Papilio14."

"What kind of name is 'Papilio,' anyway?" Jake opened the door and the boys hustled through the hallway.

"It's 'butterfly' in Latin. I assume that whoever Papilio is, they like insects. They sure do *bug* me."

"Ugh! Friends don't let friends make bad jokes," Jake laughed.

"Couldn't resist. Sorry," Ben said as they joined the medley of students flowing into the music room.

"Hey, not bad," Jake commented. The room had a tiered floor arranged in a half circle, allowing each member of the orchestra a clear view of the conductor and vice versa. Wood paneling trimmed the room.

They spotted Natalie sitting in the violin section's first-chair position. As they approached, Jake noticed his name on the second chair and Ben's on the third.

"Hi, guys," Natalie called.

They took their seats and unboxed their instruments. The conductor entered the room and the students stopped talking. He was tall with salt-and-pepper hair and wore blue jeans, a navy turtleneck sweater, and a matching sports coat. Striding confidently to the front of the orchestra, he said in a strong, welcoming voice, "Good morning, everyone! I'm Maestro Mancini."

A murmur rippled through the orchestra. *Maestro Mancini. Whoa.* Jake looked at Ben, whose eyes were also wide open. Maestro Mancini was one of the most famous living conductors, having led the London Symphony, Boston Symphony, and Leningrad Philharmonic. "This should be *great*," Jake murmured out of the corner of his mouth.

"By the expressions on your faces, I see my arrival is a surprise," Mancini said, grinning. "Your original instructor had a family emergency and I happened to be between projects, so here we are. I'm glad to be with you."

Over the next two hours, the Maestro ran each section through a series of drills and scales. As they approached dinnertime, Jake found himself drenched in sweat, partly from the physical motion of playing the violin, but mostly from stress. The Maestro had an amazing ability to hear specific people, regardless of where he was standing. He had also memorized every single person's name and position; he was able to call on each of them with ease.

Jake had played the wrong note once, and the Maestro had heard it even though he was in the back of the room helping the timpani players. Tough but fair, he had a way of correcting people without belittling them. The Maestro walked back to the front of the room. "Folks, that was good—really solid work. I was assured that you were some of the most talented students for your age. Now, hearing you, I believe it's true. However, you can always be better. I've found that you can never learn too much. I absorb something new each day from each person. You know how?"

Jake, along with a hundred other students, slowly shook his head back and forth.

"I listen. I listen to each person, whether it is a new student or a grand master. We all have something to teach and we all have something to learn. If you stop learning, your talent peaks. If you keep learning, you keep getting better. Okay, enough lecturing. I can see the hungry eyes and hear the stomachs rumbling in the front row here. It must be time for dinner."

The kids giggled and started packing up their instruments.

Chapter 9

Monday Afternoon (December 22nd)

Despite the intensity of the session, Jake felt renewed by the Maestro's comments. *I hope Julie is having as good a time as we are.* "Maestro's right. I'm starved," Jake said to Ben as they walked toward the door.

"I could eat an entire challah!" Ben replied.

Jake chuckled. He'd actually seen Ben do that on multiple occasions. As they passed the Maestro, the man reached out to grasp Ben's arm.

"Mr. Meyers," he said.

"Yes, sir?" Ben stopped.

"I had the pleasure of conducting your brother once. A remarkable musician."

"Thank you, sir," Ben said.

"I see the camp organizers placed you as third chair. As I listened to you, I could tell you belong in first chair. I'll change the order."

"No, sir. I believe it's right. I'm not as good as my friend Jake, here, or Natalie. She is very good." Ben stepped backward as if he were about to run.

"You're too modest, Mr. Meyers. Why don't you play the solo part during the holiday concert at the Navy Pier and then everyone will realize you should be in first chair." Maestro

Mancini had a persuasive style that made you want to agree with everything he said.

"Okay," squeaked Ben.

Once clear of the music room, Ben started a nervous rant about his skill and the colossal embarrassment he'd feel when he had to play a solo in front of a large crowd. "And what about Natalie? She'll think I'm trying to steal her slot," Ben concluded.

Jake grabbed his arm and drew him into a doorway in order to avoid the masses swarming into the hall. "Listen, Ben. You are good—you are great, in fact—better than I am."

"Thanks, Jake, but I know my place."

"No, you don't. I sit right next to you. Nobody can hear you as well as I can. Your notes are crisper and your draws are more complete than mine. You're better than I am but, to be candid, you freeze up during solos, so you were put in third chair."

"Thanks . . . I think." Ben studied his feet.

"What I'm trying to say is that you could be the best. It's like those really smart students who flunk tests. It's not because they don't know the material. It's because they don't test well. You need to practice solos in front of people. Come on, let's eat." Jake dragged Ben into the dining hall.

Halfway through the serving line, Jake received a text from Julie letting them know where she was sitting. They spotted Natalie and motioned for her to follow them. Julie had carefully spread her belongings out in order to save spots for everyone. Several boys had been edging closer to her and were crestfallen when Julie warmly greeted her friends.

"How did orchestra go?" Julie asked, as she bit into a grilled cheese sandwich.

"Great—Maestro Mancini is our teacher! He was a last-minute substitution," Jake replied.

"Wow—even *I've* heard of *him.*"

"How was gymnastics?" Jake asked.

"*Fantastico*, but intimidating. There are a lot of really talented girls here," Julie said.

"You'll be fine," Ben reassured her.

Julie gave Ben a sweet smile, causing him to blush.

"Ben's right. You always do well under pressure," Jake said.

"Unlike me. According to McGreevy, I crack under it." Ben jabbed his fork at a grape on his dish, but the grape squirted away and rolled across the table. "See. I can't even eat."

Natalie looked up from her soup. "Listen, maybe what you need is a place to practice in front of an audience. Have you ever thought about going to a retirement home—you know, an assisted-living residence? I play for my grandfather's place every week. It's terrific! The seniors love it and it's *super* low-pressure."

"That's a great idea!" Jake replied.

"It's a terrible idea," Ben said.

CLICK-CLICK. Jake swiveled to see Dean Stanley walking down the nearby aisle.

"Dean Stanley!" Jake shouted and stood up.

"Yes, Mr. McGreevy?" Dean Stanley closed the gap between them with surprising speed.

"Ben and I don't have any scheduled practice time tomorrow afternoon and would like to spread some holiday cheer. Is there a senior citizens' home nearby where we could play?" Jake asked.

Dean Stanley cocked his head and squinted.

Great. He probably thinks I'm pulling a fast one.

"Well, that's a thoughtful gesture. As a matter of fact, I *am* familiar with one. I'll have someone drive you there after lunch tomorrow." The Dean and his umbrella clicked off in the direction of some students tossing food around.

"Why'd you go and do that?"

"I thought I'd get us committed before you could weasel out," Jake replied.

"Committed is right—I'm committing *you* to the loony bin for thinking I'm playing a solo in front of strangers."

"Oh, stop. You'll be great. Is everyone done? I'd like to explore a bit before heading to our rooms," Jake said.

The others nodded and followed Jake to load their trays onto a motorized belt that transported their dirty dishes to the kitchen. They climbed the stone steps to the second floor, where a set of large mahogany doors opened into a remarkable library with inviting upholstered chairs. The luxurious carpet that edged the center oak floor, as well as the tables and bookshelves, seemed to suggest historic London rather than more newly minted Chicago.

"The Kenneth Matthews Library. Impressive for a room that's obsolete," Ben muttered.

"Hey, that's not nice," Jake responded.

"I can understand the charm of this place. But I think Ben is right. A library just doesn't seem that practical anymore," Natalie chimed in.

An enigma. Just when I think she's perfect for me, she says something like that. Jake padded between the aisles, soaking in the smell and the feel of the old books.

"Come on. We'd better get out of here before Jake finds some obscure book on architecture and is lost forever," Julie kidded.

"I did notice one thing," Jake said.

"Here we go!" Ben rolled his eyes.

"It's not about architecture." Jake swatted Ben's arm. "The library is named for 'Kenneth Matthews.' According to the brochure, this is the only major room in the building not named after a Stanley."

"Thank you for that scintillating report," Ben said, pretending to speak into a microphone before his television audience.

"Okay, enough teasing. Let's continue our tour, Jake," Julie said, pulling on his arm. "*Per favore*, lead the way."

They wandered through the remaining public areas, including the art room and several standard classrooms, and even found a swimming pool. Winding up their tour in the gymnasium, Julie picked up a bamboo stick from the equipment shelf. It was twenty-one inches long and had sixteen feet of multi-colored satin ribbon affixed to one end. She leapt into the air, creating spirals in front of her. But then, the ribbon became knotted.

"Argh! I can never get this right," Julie said.

"I thought it was beautiful," Natalie replied.

"Thanks. I'm okay at the more physical aspects, like leaping, but I just don't have the artistry for these maneuvers." Julie flung the stick onto the floor in disgust.

"Another demerit for Ms. O'Brien." The Dean suddenly appeared behind them. "It's against school policy to use gym equipment without supervision."

"It's just a ribbon stick," Julie responded, as she stood rigid.

"It's a violation of policy. A lack of discipline. I may have granted your father's wish for a separate room, but that's as far as I go. While you're here, you will follow my rules."

"It was my fault. I goaded her into doing it." Jake stepped in front of Julie, as if to shield her.

"Fine then. One demerit for you *and* for her." With that, the Dean swiveled and disappeared back down the hall, his umbrella clicking on the floor as he went.

"Lack of discipline? Seriously, who is this guy? My parents have rules, but even they wouldn't care about *this*." Julie huffed as she placed the stick onto the rack.

Jake squeezed her shoulder. "We'll figure something out, right, Ben?"

"We won't let you down." Ben's voice cracked a bit.

"Thanks, guys. Let's get back to our rooms before I cause all of us to get a hat trick of demerits today."

Chapter 10

Monday Evening (December 22nd)

After they returned to their room, Ben headed straight for his video game, while Jake searched the Internet on his smartphone for "Mary Cassatt 1893 World's Fair" and clicked on the first link.

"To honor the 400th anniversary of Christopher Columbus's voyage to North America, Chicago hosted the 1893 Columbian Exposition World's Fair. The fair lasted six months and its attractions were spread over 630 acres. Many of the buildings housed important achievements in industry, art, and science. The Woman's Building, dedicated to celebrating the accomplishments of women artists, poets, and educators, was a very popular attraction . . . Bertha Palmer, wife of real estate mogul Potter Palmer, commissioned a massive 64- x 15-foot mural to be painted by the Impressionist Mary Cassatt. Mary Cassatt (1844–1926) was an American painter who lived most of her life in France. Befriended by the famous Impressionist group, she was one of only a few American painters to work with the well-known artists of her time, such as Monet, Renoir, and Degas. Known to be part of the women's suffrage movement, Cassatt struggled to gain popularity within her home country, as her topics and style were often controversial." The mural, Jake learned, was hung inside the Woman's Building but disappeared fourteen years later.

Jake bit his bottom lip and thought for a moment before opening his mother's notebook.

Chapter 11

Thirteen Years Earlier (continued)

After dropping her luggage off at the Blackstone Hotel, Karen walked up South Michigan Avenue toward the museum. The trees blossoming on the street's divider heralded the new spring season. *I could have left my umbrella at the hotel.* She thought she spotted the very top of the Tribune Tower, famous for its architecture, its moon rock, and the collection of more than a hundred stones from landmarks around the world embedded in its façade. *Yes, definitely need to have Richard and Jake come out.* She hustled across E. Jackson Drive and marched up the stone steps of the Institute. Two large bronze lions, green with age, were on sentry duty, and she ducked as several families snapped photos of their children posing with one of the glorious beasts.

As instructed, she asked the security guard to page Deputy Director Royal. She didn't have to wait long before seeing a tall man with thinning brown hair bounding her way with a petite middle-aged woman by his side.

"Good morning, Ms. McGreevy. I'm Conner Royal. And may I introduce Annica Taylor. She's interning with the Institute and would like to accompany you as much as possible as you review the Cassatt."

Karen shook hands with both of them. "It's a pleasure to meet you. I would love to have some company while I work."

"And now, I'm sure you'd like to see it." Conner Royal motioned with his hands toward the entrance of the gallery.

"I can't wait." Karen followed closely behind as they traversed the museum's impressive collections. *How I would love to work in a place like* this *every day. If I handle this certification well, maybe—just maybe—I'll land that permanent position in New York I've been dreaming of.* Entering a back room, the trio went through a door with a card-key lock.

As she stepped into the room, her heart pounded with the intensity of a jackhammer. Absent-mindedly, she held her hand to her chest. *Breathe, Karen. Don't pass out now.* She rounded the corner. "Oh, my . . ." The words escaped her lips as she saw the massive painting for the first time.

"Well said," Conner replied, beaming.

Spanning the entire length of the room and lit with a special blend of incandescent and low-wattage halogen lights, the mural commanded the attention of anyone in its presence.

While the mural had water damage in several places, and was obviously coated with a hundred years of grime, the masterfulness of Cassatt's brushstrokes was evident.

"I can't believe I'm standing here. I've searched for any clue as to where this painting could be, and despite all my hopes, I thought I would never see it. And yet, here it is." Karen wiped a small tear from her eye. "Look at me—I'm a wreck. I just . . . I just think it is so beautiful."

Annica put her hand on Karen's shoulder. "That's okay. I feel the same way. To think that this hung in the Woman's Building for thousands of young girls to see . . . and that it helped them realize that they could accomplish anything. Even Susan B. Anthony understood the power of women's art, as captured by the Cassatt mural. She advocated for women's art to be displayed at the World's Fair and even spoke there. I like to think that Cassatt's work inspired many in the suffrage movement."

Karen paced the entire sixty-four feet and then returned to the two of them. "As much as I want to stare at it all day, you're not paying me to gaze at it like a schoolgirl fawning over the high school quarterback."

"That's quite all right, Ms. McGreevy."

"Karen, please."

"Very well. And do call me Conner. You take all the time you need. The Institute wants to be assured that it's purchasing the genuine article."

"It's in remarkable condition, considering it was lost for a hundred years." Karen set her bag down and crossed her arms as she evaluated the masterpiece.

"Indeed. Other than the damage along the edges and that one spot in the middle, the painting is nearly perfect. A bit dirty but nothing our techs can't handle," he replied.

"What steps have you taken to verify authenticity?" Karen asked.

"IR spectroscopic analysis, as well as measurement of the desiccation of the binder. All check out to be materials from the late nineteenth century," Annica said.

"Which firm did the analysis?" Karen asked.

"Watson and Little," Conner replied.

Karen nodded. "Yes, a small and relatively unknown company. I had the pleasure of working with them once before."

"We normally use a different firm, but we needed speed and they were able to meet our deadline. We hope to have the exhibit open to the public before the end of the year," Conner said.

"We've also had stylistic evaluations completed by an expert with the National Gallery in Washington, D.C.," Annica interjected.

"Rupert Jamison, I assume?"

"Yes, we were his last client. So sad," Conner replied.

"I heard about his death. Accidently fell in front of a Metro train in Washington?" Karen said, shaking her head.

"Yes, a real shame. He had just finished his report for the museum committee, but we thought, since you're here, you could also review the style. It can't possibly hurt to have another pair of eyes on this important acquisition. We were unable to ask Rupert any questions after he filed, so the more corroboration we have, the better," Conner said.

"I've studied Cassatt since I was a girl. I would love to do that for you. Besides, it's a great excuse to spend more time with it." Karen's cheeks warmed. *Stop it, Karen. This is just another job. Ignore the fact that you've been pursuing this mural for years.*

"Thank you. One can never have too many eyes on something for which they're about to invest $10 million dollars."

"But no pressure!" Karen exclaimed, and the others chuckled at her joke.

"Are you hungry? We could get an early lunch. And then I thought you and I would spend the afternoon reviewing the painting," Annica offered.

"No, thank you. I don't think I could eat just yet. Go ahead, please, if you like. I'll stay here." Karen spotted a stool and dragged it into the center of the room.

Conner and Annica excused themselves and left Karen alone with the mural. *Wish I could send a picture to Richard. If he and Jake can visit, maybe the museum will let them come here. Richard hates crowds. So if he could just see this mural now . . .* Karen knew that once the mural was on exhibit, the wait time to see it would be measured in hours for months to come. She giggled at the thought of Richard navigating through the waves of people who would come to see the mural. *The*

farther out to sea he is on his sailboat, the happier he seems to be.
I wonder if Jake will grow to love sailing, too.

* * *

"Jake, we overslept!" Ben hollered.

Jake woke up with a start as Ben nudged him, his eyes darting to his watch.

George Barrie's drawing of the central figures
from the middle panel of Mary Cassatt's mural

Chapter 12

Tuesday Morning (December 23rd)

Uh-oh, it's 5:55 already! Only five minutes until we're supposed to be lined up in the gym. "I'm awake, I'm awake."

"Here, I grabbed some clothes for you. You can't show up in what you had on yesterday. Too wrinkled." Ben tossed him some black slacks and a red button-down shirt. The camp had a strict *no jeans in class* policy. Hair a mess, teeth still fuzzy, and smelling like he'd been on a bus trip the entire previous day, Jake wasn't thrilled with his appearance for the first full day of camp. His shoes squeaked on the rubberized mat as he lined up next to Ben. Five seconds later, the bell rang.

"Good morning," Dean Stanley bellowed as his umbrella tip thudded against the floor.

"Good morning," a half-hearted and still-asleep crowd responded.

"Not what I expected." The Dean's face soured. "My staff assured me you'd be special—that you were hand-chosen and the best of your class. Yet you show up this morning with such lackluster focus and discipline. It's disappointing . . . mighty disappointing, I must say." The Dean paused when he reached Jake's row.

"And it appears some of you didn't even bother to explore our superb showering facilities." His withering glare struck deep. *The Dean's right. I'm normally more put together than this.*

After hearing the day's agenda, the students were released

to breakfast. Jake skipped the line, grabbing a banana on the way, and headed for the third floor to shower and clean up before their morning music session. The bathroom was indeed excellent, as the Dean had said. Jake normally hated public showers and avoided using them at all costs. But these showers were each individually walled off with private changing areas. He spent more time than usual washing away the past thirty-six hours, as well as reflecting on his mom's notebook, which mostly detailed her search over the years for the missing Cassatt. The timer on his watch beeped and Jake reluctantly turned the water off.

"Thanks for waking me up and getting my clothes out this morning," Jake said when he met Ben in the hallway.

"No problem. We're lucky that I woke up." Ben followed Jake into the music room.

"Papilio14?" Jake arched an eyebrow.

"Yeah. They were online last night trying to pad their lead. I had to keep pace in building and planting or my village would never produce enough gardens to match their output," Ben explained. "But then some new player decided to fly a crop duster over my fields and killed my plants!"

"You can do that? Seems mean," Jake responded.

"You're not supposed to be able to do that, but whoever it was found a loophole or something. Actually, it was quite ingenious."

"Think it was Papilio14?"

"No, they would have attacked me long ago. But my lands are strong enough that this person only momentarily frustrated me," Ben replied.

"Seems like a lot of energy just for pride," Jake said.

"Oh, there's more than pride on the line. Whoever can amass the most points by the end of the contest wins a custom game room."

Natalie was once again already in her chair warming up.

"Hi, Natalie." Jake cringed at the exuberance in his voice.

"Good morning, Jake, Ben," Natalie said, nodding to the boys.

"Sleep okay?" Jake asked. *I'm lousy at small talk. Why is this so hard?*

"I struggle to sleep in new places. My mind's too active," Natalie replied.

"Might be because you're smart. I've read that many intelligent people hardly sleep at all," Jake said. "I think I remember reading that Ben Franklin was a bit of a night owl."

"A sleeping fox catches no poultry." Natalie smiled and cute dimples formed in the sides of her cheek.

She just quoted Ben Franklin. A tingle shot up Jake's spine.

*   *   *

After the grueling but educational morning session, Jake and Ben gobbled down lunch and headed for the front door. Armed with his violin case and trusty backpack, Jake followed his friend as he climbed into the Stanley House transport van. Much to Jake's disappointment, they didn't pass any famous Chicago landmarks. Instead, they saw only snow-covered sidewalks and boring brick townhouses. The van turned up a driveway leading to a structure with an overhang to protect arriving guests from the elements. The building jutted off at forty-five-degree angles on both sides.

"I'll be back in two hours," the driver, a middle-aged man with a rapidly receding hairline, said. Jake gave him a thumbs-up and slammed the van door. He shivered when the bitter winter wind nipped his ears.

"I didn't think it would be so cold here," Ben chattered through his teeth as he trudged up the walk.

"It's the lake-effect wind. Brings moisture from Lake Michigan and makes it feel colder than it really is," Jake replied.

"Whatever, weatherman McGreevy," Ben muttered.

He must be nervous. Ben's not normally so touchy. Jake tried opening the large door but it was locked. He pressed the buzzer located on the side.

"May I help you?" a voice squawked from the tiny speaker sunken into the wall.

"We're from Stanley House. We're here to play some music for the residents," Jake replied.

A bell rang and Jake heard the lock click. He stepped through the door and into a large welcome area. Holiday garlands decorated the walls and the wooden counter area of the reception desk. A medium-sized Christmas tree wrapped in red and green lights twinkled in the corner. On the other side of the room, a festive blue-and-white display table of dreidels, Hanukkah gelt, and Jewish stars surrounded an iron menorah. A box of kinara candles was being unpacked by a staff member on another nearby table for the Kwanza display. Worn maroon carpet covered the floors. The vaulted ceiling housed several large skylights, letting some of the grayish sun pour into the lobby. Jake paused to stare at several gallon-sized empty paint cans sitting on the floor under the edges of the skylights.

"My brother, a building contractor, likes to say that there are two kinds of skylights: those that leak and those that will. That's why the cans are here. You must be Jake and Ben," a woman's voice called.

Jake turned to see an older woman approaching them.

"I'm Hannah. I run the residents' committee." She offered her hand to the boys. Hannah had surprisingly smooth dark skin and only a hint of silver in her hair. If not for the fact that she wasn't wearing a staff member's uniform, Jake would have never guessed she was a resident.

"Jake, Jake McGreevy. This is my friend Ben Meyers."

The boys each shook her hand. Jake was impressed with the strength he felt when she gripped his.

"My, your hands are cold. Have you no mittens, young man?" Hannah asked.

"I forgot them in New York." Jake felt himself blushing.

"Well, that simply won't do. You can't play the violin with hands as cold as ice. Come with me. We'll get you some hot cocoa. That'll warm you up." Hannah led them to a seating area that held a coffee pot and a hot-water dispenser.

"This might appear to be simple instant cocoa, but I assure you it's a special blend—a recipe handed down from my grandmother." Hannah measured and poured various shades of brown powder and sugar into two mugs and filled them with hot water. She stirred the ingredients with a spoon, dropped in some miniature marshmallows, and presented the drinks to the boys.

Jake took a sip and grinned. "This *is delicious!*" Jake and Ben looked at each other and smiled. Most of their friends were into fancy coffees, but they preferred classic cocoa to overpriced java.

Chapter 13

Tuesday Afternoon (December 23rd)

"Was I right? Nothing hits the spot quite like cocoa," Hannah said, carrying their empty mugs to the sink. "Now that you're nice and toasty, please, follow me. I'd like to show you around." Hannah padded down the hallway.

The boys stashed their violins below the reception counter and fell in line behind her.

Jake tried not to stare into the rooms as he passed. Many doors were open, with TVs blaring out seemingly random noise.

"Here's the day room. Most of the action can be found here." Hannah motioned with her arm like a champion tour guide.

The dayroom was spacious, with floor-to-ceiling windows. On the left, several couches and chairs formed a semicircle around a dated rear-projection television. Nearby was a cluster of square tables, sparsely populated with a handful of elderly people playing cards. Jake saw a resident struggling with the TV's remote control. Spurred into action, he walked over to the man. "May I help you?" he asked.

"Blasted thing. Nothing seems to work around here. I already tried to replace the batteries and it still doesn't work." The man handed the ancient remote to Jake.

Jake popped the cover off. "Here's the problem. The battery connections are corroded." Jake pulled his Leatherman multi-tool from the outer pocket on his backpack and flipped open

57

the flathead screwdriver. He scraped the greenish goo that had formed around the terminals into a nearby trash can. Replacing the cover, he handed the device back to the man.

"Hey, it works. Nice going, kid."

Jake nodded and returned to Hannah and Ben.

"Thank you for that. The remote's been driving poor Mr. Johnston crazy." Hannah rested her hand on Jake's shoulder. "Now, for some introductions. Over there, on the right. I call that the VFW." Hannah waved to a group of men playing pool. Jake observed them closely and realized that they were all wearing some sort of military baseball cap announcing their ship, battalion, or squadron.

"I get it. Veterans of Foreign Wars," Jake said, as he tried not to stare at them. In just one glance, he spotted veterans from many different conflicts. He felt humbled as he recognized hats from the USS Yorktown, 1st Marine Division, 101st Airborne, and 5th Air Force. "Some giants in history standing over there," Jake murmured.

"Well put, young man. Now on this side over here are the weavers. I call them that partly because of their knitting, but also because they weave great tales. You never know if they are true, but they are *fascinating* nonetheless."

Jake followed her arm to the right-hand corner of the room, where a group of ladies sat in easy chairs. Huge balls of yarn littered the floor and their needles clicked in unison.

DING! DING! DING!

Jake was startled by the piercing ring of an alarm. He saw Hannah move swiftly to a nearby emergency exit where a resident had approached the door. Hannah steered the woman around and back to her seat. Two orderlies, responding to the sound, turned and left as the buzzing stopped.

"What's going on?" he asked as Hannah returned.

"Some of the more senior people here have tracking

devices on them. Whenever they get near a door, the sensor sends out a warning. We don't want them to wander away."

"Cool. Kind of a security feature, so families know that their parents or grandparents will be safe."

"Precisely."

The wheels in Jake's mind churned and he glanced at Ben.

"Dean Stanley!" the boys whispered.

"What?" Hannah asked.

"Nothing. Do you happen to have an extra sensor lying around?" Jake asked.

"I imagine I can dig one up. You boys ready to play?"

"We'll go get our violins." Jake led the way to the reception desk. By the time they returned to the dayroom, it had been transformed into a mini concert hall. All of the chairs and couches now formed a circle around the center of the room.

"Wow, that was fast," Jake exclaimed.

"We may seem frail and slow, but most of us here still have some pep," Hannah said, beaming.

Jake and Ben sat in the middle and pulled their violins from their cases. Although no announcement had been made, Jake realized the residents were streaming into the dayroom from the adjourning hallways. *There have to be twenty people here.*

Jake leaned over to Ben. "Let's play the first half of the holiday concert: 'Jingle Bells,' 'Winter Wonderland,' 'Let It Snow,' 'Ma'oz Tzur,' 'Joy to the World,' 'Carol of the Bells,' and 'Hanukkah, Oh, Hanukkah.'"

"Okay, but you play the solo part for 'Carol of the Bells,'" Ben said.

"No, let's just both play it together instead of one of us doing a solo part," Jake replied.

"Got it." Ben's voice projected a bit of confidence.

Good. He's getting comfortable.

The boys started playing, trying not to be bothered by the fact that some of the audience members had already drifted off to sleep—and one was snoring loudly. Much like everything else Jake and Ben did, their playing was in perfect unison. The rhythm of their fingers and the strokes of their bows matched as they raced through the songs without pause. The crowd clapped and sang along, tapping their toes. Their smiles and wide eyes warmed Jake's heart.

They finished up "Joy to the World" and began the fast-paced opening section of "Carol of the Bells." Jake lifted his bow from the strings and lowered it by his side. He saw the rapid dirty glance from Ben. He almost felt bad about tricking Ben into playing the solo, but as he watched his friend attack the strings, he knew he'd made the right decision. *Ben's so good—if only he could see that.*

Beads of sweat formed along Ben's hairline. He missed a couple of strokes but nobody in the crowd so much as blinked, mesmerized as they were by the young man's performance. Jake picked up his bow and joined Ben. They finished the song and received boisterous applause.

"Mazel tov!" Jake exclaimed, using one of Ben's favorite expressions. "Really, congratulations. You did a great job."

"That was low, McGreevy." Ben half scowled and half smiled.

"Desperate measures, my friend," Jake replied. "Let's finish strong."

Ben nodded and kicked off "Hanukkah, Oh, Hanukkah."

When the boys were done, they were approached by several residents who wanted to thank them, and they stood around for another thirty minutes talking.

As they prepared to leave, Hannah offered Jake a pair of knitted mittens. "Here. These aren't as fancy as whatever fabric scientists have created for us lately, but they should keep your hands warm."

Jake accepted the pair of multicolored mittens. The yarn was a tight weave and doubled over, offering lots of protection. "These are great. Thank you very much. Did the weavers have extras or something?"

"No, my dear, they made them just now when I asked," Hannah replied.

"Amazing. That fast?"

"When you've done something for sixty years, you get pretty good at it. They're actually thinking about trying to sell them at craft fairs and such. We even put a label with our home's name inside this pair, so you won't forget us." Hannah linked her arm through Jake's and walked with him and Ben to the exit. Placing her arm around Ben, she added, "I hope you'll both come back again to see us very soon."

"You bet!" Ben's reply beat Jake's to the punch.

Chapter 14

Tuesday Afternoon (December 23rd)

"You're going to *bug* Dean Stanley?" Julie sounded worried when Jake and Ben rolled out their plan for outsmarting the Dean.

"Not bug—*track.* Hannah gave us a tracking device, and Ben thinks he can rig our cell phones to monitor his movements. It's not that we're planning to do anything wrong, but I think you'd agree it would be best for all of us to keep tabs on him," Jake explained.

"I think it's great. Very James Bond–like," Natalie said.

"It will probably take me a while to program it, but I like the challenge," Ben said.

"Does the sensor use Wi-Fi or Bluetooth protocol, or will you have to manipulate it—perhaps a broad-spectrum scan using the frequency modulator in the phone?" Natalie asked.

Jake clenched his jaw, trying not to swivel and give Ben the *Whoa* look. He could sense Ben was resisting the same urge.

"I, ah, I'm not quite sure yet." Ben stumbled over his words. "I, well . . ."

"I'm sure Ben will come up with *something* clever," Jake interjected.

"I'm not sure why I hang out with you, McGreevy. You seem to attract trouble." Julie crossed her arms.

"I suppose it's my good looks and charm that keep you around. But remember, you have two demerits, and I have just one."

"That's true. And you are kind of cute." She winked at him, causing him to shiver. *Do I still have feelings for her?* "How'd your afternoon go?"

"Just peachy! My instructor recommended that I not hold the stick so tight in order to let the ribbon flow better, but then it slipped out of my hand and flew across the room. It was horrible."

"I'm sure it wasn't *that* bad," Natalie consoled.

"Samantha had this smug look on her face when I finished. She then did the same routine perfectly and made a remark to the instructor about how easy it was," Julie fumed.

"I wish there weren't bullies, but I imagine there always will be," Jake lamented.

"As long as there are people with low confidence who need to feel superior, there will be bullies," Natalie said.

"I don't have any confidence and you don't see me bullying anyone," Ben half joked.

"Perhaps a *disciplined approach* to practicing will solve your problem, Julie." Jake spoke in a low baritone similar to Dean Stanley's.

"Right, as long as I'm not *too* lackluster about it," Julie responded as she stiffened her posture.

Everyone laughed.

"Seriously, why do you think the Dean is so grouchy?" Natalie asked.

"Hard to say. But when I researched the person that the library's named in memory of, Kenneth Matthews, I found out he had been a student here—that is, until he disappeared. That might explain the Dean's determination to keep everyone safe," Jake said.

*   *   *

After dinner, Ben went straight to work writing the code to enable them to track Dean Stanley. Jake threw himself onto his bed and pulled out his mom's notebook. Still exhausted from the bus trip and the stress of their first full day, Jake knew he should go to sleep but felt the urge to keep reading, not only to learn his mother's theories about the mural, but also to look for those infrequent personal thoughts that might help him get to know her better.

Chapter 15

Thirteen Years Earlier (continued)

After a restless night, Karen left the hotel early in the morning for the brisk walk up to the Institute. As she said good morning to the doorman, she noticed another man standing near the entrance. He had black hair parted down the middle and sported an unhealthy-looking fake tan that made his skin appear almost orange, as if he had covered his face with bronzer. *How odd.* Karen was used to seeing strange-looking people in New York City, but this man's appearance was really unsettling. Or maybe it was just the way he was looking at her. She thought about asking the doorman to hail a taxi, but when she noticed the tanned man duck into the hotel, she decided to walk.

For the second day in a row, Karen was back at the Institute at six in the morning. As she sat alone on the wooden stool, she stared at the center panel with the scene of women in an orchard. Entitled *Young Women Plucking the Fruits of Knowledge or Science*, it represented women's progression into the academic and industrial world.

The eyes—the eyes seem off. Karen approached the mural and stood on the stepladder. Now only inches away, she gazed into the eyes of the figure as if in a staring contest. *Yes, the eyes are wrong.*

"Early bird again, huh?" Annica's voice nearly knocked Karen off the ladder.

Recovering her composure, Karen turned to the woman. "Yes, I haven't been able to sleep much here. It's the first time I've been away from my son, so I'm having trouble relaxing."

"Oh, I can certainly understand that. Any concerns so far?"

"It's an extraordinary work of art. There is almost too much to take in. I can see why Rupert took a month. Even then, he was probably rushing."

"You sound conflicted. Do you think there's a problem?" Annica asked.

"Well, I do find the eyes on these women to be odd. In Cassatt's similar painting, *Young Women Picking Fruit,* the eyes have a much different appearance—an almost regal air about them. These eyes are cold and distant, not what I would expect for the scene she's portraying."

Annica stepped closer and peered up at the painting. "You're talking about the painting at the Carnegie in Pittsburgh, right? I grew up loving that painting. My grandparents lived in Baldwin, just south of Pittsburgh, so I visited many times. But didn't she do that painting earlier? Maybe she decided to go with a more determined expression and it just comes off a bit cold, as you said?"

"Perhaps that's it. Or maybe I just need more caffeine."

"Come on. The café doesn't open for a few hours, but the security guards have a pot brewing all the time and it isn't too bad. This way." Annica motioned with her arm.

"Sounds good. Can we swing by Conner's office on the way back? He's going to give me the documentation from the other certifiers so that I can wrap a bow around the provenance case."

"Sure," Annica said as she led Karen toward the exit.

"How are you enjoying your internship?" Karen asked.

"I love it. I'm hoping to secure a permanent position here. I tried painting but I wasn't ever able to break into the galleries. So instead, I took night classes while working and eventually earned my degree. The Institute was kind enough to hire me a few months ago."

"It was really courageous of you to go back to school. I truly admire you for that."

* * *

Conner handed Karen a two-inch-thick stack of papers. When she settled into an office to review the documents, she had to resist the urge to go back to the painting. Normally, she loved plowing through paperwork, but the eyes in the painting were haunting her. *Keep moving forward, Karen.* Thirty minutes later, when she reached the summary page from the Watson and Little report, a nagging feeling overtook her. She fired up her laptop and navigated to the Watson and Little folder she had saved from a previous job. Using a trick she'd learned from a friend, she inverted the page on the screen. She then inverted the paper in her hand and compared the curvature of the signature on the screen to the one from the Art Institute. Both documents were signed by Gerald Watson, but the signatures were different from one another. A chill slithered down Karen's spine and she wrapped her arms around herself for warmth.

"Are you cold? It tends to get a little chilly in here, but, as you know, canvasses like cooler consistent temperatures." Conner Royal's booming voice startled Karen. She hadn't heard him approach and was surprised to see that both he and Annica were standing behind her.

She quickly closed her laptop and shoved the report into the stack of papers. "Maybe a little. I was just thinking I needed to wrap up for the day. My head is spinning from reading so many technical reports. Tomorrow I'll get back to the painting itself."

*   *   *

When she returned to her room, she searched for a news article on her computer discussing Rupert Jamison's death. She finally found one that highlighted a quote from the investigator, Detective O'Malley: "We did briefly look at a murder angle. It was a very strange accident. However, we couldn't find any suspects and the forensics were inconclusive."

Scrolling to the end of the article, Karen noticed an "update" link, which she immediately clicked. The date was two days after the last report. An eyewitness said that she had seen a man with very tan skin trip near the edge of the tracks, causing a domino effect, resulting in Rupert Jamison's fatal fall. Without more to go on—the accident occurred at rush hour, so the cameras were not able to pick up any other helpful details—the case was ruled an accident.

Karen's heart sank. *Could the tanned man outside my hotel and the man seen at the Metro be one and the same?*

*   *   *

The next morning, Karen resumed her review of the painting and worked for several hours before taking a break. While sitting at her desk, she decided to revisit the details of the discovery. She'd already confirmed that the building where the mural was found was once owned by Hiram Sibley. Although not his primary warehouse, it had been one of the assets of his company. This was significant, as many of the artifacts from the World's Fair had been stored in Sibley's warehouse, and that fact lent credibility to the find. *Why didn't anyone find the mural in the warehouse before now?* Karen logged into her all-access account for nearly every public database in the country. Finding the Chicago real estate records page, she started tracing the owners of the warehouse since

Hiram's family sold it in 1939. Since then, it had changed hands three times. During World War II the warehouse had been used as a storage depot for the government. *Easy for it to be ignored during that time period.* The next owner was a large automotive distributor, and as far as Karen could tell, the company never utilized the warehouse. When Karen reviewed the bill of sale transferring the property from the automotive company to the current owner, she slid back in her chair as if her computer were poisoned. The bill of sale included the new owner's address at the time the transaction took place: Baldwin, Pennsylvania.

Baldwin—where Annica's family is from? "She couldn't be—" Karen gasped.

"Still gawking like a kid looking at the Macy's Christmas display?" Conner asked.

"Yes, I guess so. I . . . I actually think I need a break," Karen stammered, trying to recover from being startled and from this most disturbing revelation. "I'm going to go for a walk if that's okay."

"Sure. I'll tell Annica you left early. I know she's interested in discussing some of the analysis reports with you, but it can wait," Conner said.

Wanting to clear her head and think of anything but the painting, she stepped into the museum gift shop and picked up a soft, cuddly bear with "The Art Institute of Chicago" embroidered on its blue T-shirt. She smiled and carried it to the counter.

Sifting through the contents of her purse, she reached past the miniature Leatherman multi-tool Richard had given her and a small sewing kit, and found her wallet. After paying for the toy, she walked out of the museum and its perfectly controlled temperature. Her cell phone chirped when she left the stone-walled building. Due to the weak signal inside the museum, she had missed the call. Pausing in the doorway, she triggered the playback of the voicemail.

With Jake's favorite kids' tune playing loudly in the background, the message played: "Hi, honey! How's everything? Jake and I are having a wonderful day inside. It's raining. But tomorrow promises to be sunny, and we have big plans to go to the zoo, right, Jakey? No, no, Jake, don't press that button on the mixer! Uh-oh! Here, say hello to Mommy." Karen heard her son's high voice next: "Hi, Mommy! We're having fun!" Jake giggled. "Okay, Karen," Richard said. "Call me back as soon as you can. We love you and miss you very much!"

Not knowing what to do, Karen started walking north on Michigan Avenue. She dialed Richard but got his voicemail. *I need to talk to someone. This can't really be happening. Forgeries happen all the time, but I just didn't think I would ever see one! This is horrible. Richard, pick up your phone!* she thought as she listened to ring after ring. Finally, the phone was answered, but instead of Richard's voice, she heard an automated voice say, "The subscriber's mailbox you have reached is full. Please try again." *I keep telling Richard he has to delete old messages. How can he be so brilliant yet so careless?*

She crossed Michigan and started down Randolph Street. Checking for oncoming cars, she noticed a man walking behind her. *Bronzer—the man from outside the hotel. He's behind me!* Fear pulsed through her veins. *Could this really be the guy the witness saw in the D.C. Metro station? Did he kill Rupert because he discovered the Cassatt was a forgery? Is he after me now?*

When she reached State Street, she turned up toward the Chicago Theatre. A bustling crowd was flowing in for the midafternoon matinee. She peeked back, hoping not to see Bronzer. *No!* Thirty feet behind her, the man was elbowing his way through the crowd.

"Sold-out show. Get the last ticket here. Last ticket—just fifty bucks." A scalper waved a theater ticket.

"Here!" Karen pulled the emergency cash she kept tucked inside her purse's side pocket and pressed it into the man's hand. Grabbing the ticket, she escaped into the lobby.

She hurried up to the second floor and found a bench to sit on. After fifteen frustrating minutes talking with the police but getting the runaround from them about evidence, restraining orders, stalking, and safety tips, she hung up the phone. Richard still didn't answer, so she called her neighbor and asked her to leave a note for him on the door to their apartment.

The second floor was eerily quiet, as all of the patrons had entered the auditorium. Karen looked up at the light sconce and noticed a loose screw protruding from it. Feeling ridiculously paranoid, she nonetheless quickly jotted something on the inside cover of her notebook. Then, she scribbled another note on a piece of paper, cut a thin hole in the bottom of the teddy bear, and stitched it up with her needle and thread. Using her Leatherman, she loosened the sconce, stuffed her notebook into the wall, and screwed the sconce back into place. Before tucking her Leatherman back into her purse, she used the tool to etch her initials into the metal on the side of the sconce.

* * *

Wednesday Morning (December 24th)

The next morning, Jake tried to hide a yawn with his violin. He hadn't finished reading his mother's notes until the wee hours of the morning. While most of the pages detailed her investigation over the years of the missing mural, the last page was dedicated to her initial impressions of her trip to Chicago:

A wonderful trip so far! The deputy director, Conner Royal, and his intern, Annica, are making the experience a real pleasure for me. They give me unlimited access to the painting! My hotel is within walking distance, which, because spring has sprung, gives me an opportunity to feel part of a vibrant city—for a few minutes anyway—just as it blossoms, before heading into work. I did experience a tense moment when a strangely tanned man seemed to be following me. Maybe it's just a nervousness I have whenever I'm away from my family—noticing everything and everyone in a hyper-alert way—or maybe it's just me—always aware of every detail—but his bronzed appearance did make me jumpy, right up until I reached those welcoming lions at the museum. I'm excited to begin my first full day of work!

Then Jake read the last entry in her notebook from later that same day:

Note to self: Check the eyes of Cassatt's earlier works. Something is off here. They are too cold, distant. Not what I'd expect. Must investigate, call colleagues, and check sources!

Maestro Mancini had already shot Jake two stern looks after previous yawns.

"You need more discipline, McGreevy," Ben muttered out of the side of his mouth, causing Jake and Natalie to giggle. Jake had been up all night pondering his mother's last thoughts and her notes on the Cassatt's potential locations—notes she'd made before she ever got the call to come to Chicago. Thankfully, he'd set his phone to ring in plenty of time to rouse Ben, who had also been up late working on the tracking device.

He'd tried to fish information from his dad earlier when he had called after breakfast. However, it was awkward to ask anything of substance about his mother, her death, or the Cassatt while talking on his cell phone in the crowded hallway.

"Mr. McGreevy, if you're done dreaming of sugar plums and jolly old St. Nick visiting tonight, tell me the bowing for 'Carol of the Bells,' third line?" The Maestro's booming voice rattled Jake. With sweat beading on his forehead, he leaned over to peer at his music.

"Don't look at it. Tell me now. The music should always be with you, engrained in your soul." Mancini's voice was sharp, but laced with passion, not anger.

Jake leaned back and said the first thing that popped into his head. "Tremolo."

"Good." The Maestro moved on and continued to discuss the logistics for tomorrow's Christmas Day concert at Winter Wonderfest on the Navy Pier.

"Dude, where did you pull that from?" Ben whispered.

"Just lucky, I guess." Jake tried to be nonchalant, but deep down, he knew the music was with him. Engrained. The Maestro's phrase triggered a memory of a discussion with his father. *We McGreevys are focused people. And when we focus on something, anything is possible. Your mother was younger than her colleagues, but I'd put her eye for art against anyone else's in the world.* An uneasy feeling twisted in his stomach. *My mom was on to something.* "It's a fake!" Jake exclaimed.

"What's fake?" Ben whispered.

Jake shook his head. "Not now. I'll tell you later."

Chapter 16

Wednesday Afternoon (December 24th)

Jake filled two tall glasses with iced tea, hoping to hydrate his way to more alertness. He was the last to reach the spot in the dining room that he, Ben, Julie, and Natalie had claimed as their regular table.

"Ben was just telling me how he got the tracking device working," said Natalie, beaming.

Jealousy momentarily spiked in Jake's mind. "Yes, he told me."

"I'll install an app I made onto each of your phones. It will play the "Imperial March" ring tone from *Star Wars* whenever Dean Stanley is nearby."

"'Imperial March?' Nice touch. So now we just have to attach it to him," Jake said.

"How are you going to do that?" Julie asked.

Jake glanced around and spotted the Dean. Reaching into his backpack, he took out a stick of gum and chewed it rapidly. "Give me the sensor," he whispered.

Ben handed him the tracking device. Normally housed within an ankle bracelet, Ben had extracted the component, leaving something the size of just two nickels glued together. Jake wrapped the gum around it and walked toward the Dean. After talking briefly with the man, he returned to his friends.

"Done."

"That fast?"

"Killed two birds with one stone. I asked if we could go to the retirement home again. I also asked if Julie and Natalie could join. He seemed to be okay with it. While we were talking, I dropped it into his umbrella. The gum should make it stick to the sides and keep it in place," Jake replied.

"Perfect, as long as it doesn't rain," Ben said.

"True, but it's winter—and that umbrella doesn't look as if it gets much use other than being the Dean's walking stick. We'll just have to see."

"Maybe the Dean's not that bad of a guy. He seems okay with our going to the retirement home," Julie said.

"Could be," Jake shrugged. "Maybe he has a soft spot for them, as he's near that age himself."

*   *   *

The school van pulled into a space at the retirement facility behind a police cruiser. *What's going on?* Jake sprinted ahead of the others up the walkway to the front door. When they were buzzed in, they saw a couple of officers talking with a staff member and Hannah.

"We're very sorry. It won't happen again," the staff member said.

"Right. That's what you say every time." The officers turned and marched out the door. Hannah's eyes sparkled when she saw Jake. "So good to see you," she said as she came over to them. "How are the mittens working out?"

"They're great. Very warm, thank you." Jake smiled, and introduced Natalie and Julie.

"What's happening here?" Ben asked.

"Oh, we have a few residents who get confused and sometimes call the police. We try to stop them, but they find their way to phones and call 911 to report thefts when things disappear. This time it was a bit more serious. Poor old Mr. Perlmutter called to say that his roommate was missing," Hannah said.

"And there isn't anything wrong with his roommate?" Julie asked.

"Heavens, no, dear. He just moved to Arizona to be closer to his family. But when Mr. Perlmutter woke up this morning and found him gone, he concluded something horrible had happened. He just plum forgot he'd said goodbye to him yesterday."

"Seems like life here is far from boring," Jake said.

"Usually, it's a tad dull, but some days, there is a bit more going on. Are you here to play for us again?" Hannah rested her hands on the boys' shoulders.

Jake checked his watch. "We thought we'd play a few songs and maybe help wrap gifts or decorate—whatever you think would be most helpful."

Hannah escorted them back to the dayroom. Jake, Ben, and Natalie played the most upbeat pieces in their repertoire, and Julie practiced some of her gymnastic routines. Nothing fancy, just some cartwheels and twirls, but the residents clapped as if it were the Olympics. When they finished playing, since this was Natalie and Julie's first visit, Hannah showed them around the building. The amenities were pretty nice and most seniors seemed to be happy. *I know people don't want to leave their homes, but this doesn't seem too bad. It's like living at a college dorm, but without all the studying.*

Jake and his friends then enjoyed another cup of Hannah's excellent cocoa while waiting to be picked up.

*   *   *

The kids' cell phones simultaneously chirped the "Imperial March" as the van neared the school. The Dean was standing in the cold waiting for them.

"Mr. McGreevy, I need you to come with me."

Jake's pulse pounded. *What now?*

Chapter 17

Wednesday Afternoon (December 24th)

"Step lively. We have people waiting for you." The Dean motioned with his hand to hurry Jake along.

Confusion replaced fear as Jake's chief emotion. He shot a glance to Ben, who returned a similarly bewildered look. Once inside the school, Jake understood. A local television crew had positioned its spotlight so that any interviewee would have the oversized Stanley House crest as the backdrop.

I should have expected some showboating from the Dean. Jake had received a good deal of unwanted celebrity after his adventure in Ireland, but he had hoped that was all behind him. Apparently not. At least by now he was conditioned to answer the standard array of questions reporters liked to ask when doing human-interest stories.

"Hi, Jake. Layna Smith, Channel 6 News. I was here filming a piece on the Sound in Motion intensive program and the holiday fundraising concerts you will perform. When I learned you were participating, I wanted to ask you a few questions." A young woman in her mid-twenties offered her hand.

"Sure," Jake responded, combing his hair absently with his hands. Thankfully, the school's strict dress code meant he was at least presentable and didn't have the normal just-rolled-out-of-bed look. Jake stood in front of the crest and waited for his eyes to adjust to the glare from the camera's lights.

Layna faced the camera. "Good afternoon. Many of us have already spent too much and will go into debt this Christmas.

However, for one clever teen, shopping this year shouldn't be a problem. I'm here with Jake McGreevy, the youth who last summer captured the Irish "Midweek Bandits" and found missing treasure amounting to hundreds of millions of dollars. He's here in Chicago for a specialized music program."

What was it like when you first found the treasure? Jake recited one of the typical questions in his mind.

"Jake, when you first stumbled upon the treasure, how did you feel? What was it like?" Layna verbally echoed Jake's thoughts. Without missing a beat, Jake provided the well-rehearsed response. "It's difficult to characterize. It was a rush of energy mixed with a surreal feeling, like a dream almost."

You placed yourself in harm's way for your friends. What was going through your mind?

"And when you confronted the crooks, what were you thinking about?" the reporter asked, and Jake promptly answered her question.

What did you do with the money you received from the treasure? Jake waited for that next question.

"You're in Chicago, the city where your mother was brutally run down. Considering the driver responsible was never caught and could be out there today watching, what would you like to say to that person?" Layna tilted the microphone closer to Jake.

Dumbfounded by the sudden changeup in questions, Jake visibly stepped backward. *I can't believe she asked that.* Thoughts collided in his mind like bumper cars. He glanced over at Julie, who was in shock. Jake could see tears forming in her eyes.

Stay strong, Jake. Fueled by newfound courage, Jake faced the camera. "I'll never know my mother. If the driver has a shred of decency, he'll turn himself in."

Jake tuned out Layna as she closed the story by discussing

tomorrow's Christmas Day concert and other planned school outings, including trips to the Art Institute and Museum of Science and Industry. The entire experience left Jake exhausted. His friends rushed up as soon as the cameraman turned off the spotlight.

"That was terrible. I can't believe she asked you that," Ben said.

Julie hugged him, the warmth of her embrace bringing him out of his stupor. "I agree: That was horrible. My dad says you have to watch out for young reporters. They're always trying to make a name for themselves and will cruelly push the limits of civility," Julie said in a tone loud enough to ensure Layna heard it.

Jake silently applauded Julie's attempt to insult the reporter. "It's okay. I just never thought about what I'd say to the person who killed my mom . . ."

*   *   *

They joined the crowd flowing into the dining hall. Jake chose vegetable soup with beans and pasta, hoping the warm, thick mixture would comfort him. They ate in silence, as the reporter had dampened their mood.

"Well, if it isn't Sasquatch and her goofy sidekicks." Samantha's voice cut the air.

Before Jake could answer, Julie stood up and towered over her gymnastic rival. "Sasquatch is a mythical being. Keep pushing me and you'll find I'm plenty real."

Jake smiled, pleased to see Julie standing up for herself.

Dah-dah-dah da ta-da da ta-da. The "Imperial March" ring tone sounded once on each of their phones. Julie and the others sat down and tried to ignore Samantha.

"What's going on here?" Dean Stanley arrived moments later and directed the question to Jake and his friends, all but ignoring Samantha.

"Dean Stanley, this girl was threatening me." Samantha pointed at Julie.

Julie's face turned crimson. "That's not true. You're the one who came over here to insult *me*," Julie stammered.

"Me? I was just offering some pointers on your ribbon exercise to be helpful." The ease and speed with which Samantha came up with a bald-faced lie sent a chill up Jake's spine. *This girl's a sociopath.*

"Ms. O'Brien, as you cannot afford more demerits, I'll offer you a deal. Report to the gym now and help the staff rearrange the equipment and I'll ignore your transgression here." The Dean's tone left no room for argument. Julie started to speak but stopped after Jake shook his head in a brief but purposeful *No*.

"Yes, sir. Gladly," Julie said.

Chapter 18

Wednesday Evening (December 24th)

Despite the fact that Jake and Ben helped Julie with her chores in the gym, they still took more than an hour to finish. Jake collapsed onto his bed, grateful for the comfort of the plush mattress. *The Dean might be an ogre on discipline, but he sure knows how to furnish a school.*

"Aren't you tired?" Jake asked Ben, who was booting up his game.

"Papilio14 is still ahead of me, and someone pranked me again. This time they diverted a river and flooded my barn, causing my dairy cows to get stuck in the mud."

Jake snickered.

"I'd think you were the culprit, since that's your modus operandi, but I know you've been focused on your mom," Ben said.

He's right. I can't stop wondering who she was or what happened. What would I say to the person who killed my mom? A variety of unpleasant words and thoughts cascaded through his mind, but he realized this wasn't a movie. *There are no clever lines to say. I just want him caught. She obviously sensed the danger, because she stashed the notebook in the wall behind the sconce and sewed the note inside the bear. When she was hit, she was clutching the bear. The police must have given it to my father.*

Jake tried to organize the people and the events detailed in his mother's notes. Rupert, Annica, Conner—all the names swirled in his head. He needed to think the way his mom would, but Layna's question gnawed at him and he found himself filled with rage. Loneliness quickly replaced the anger and he started to feel sorry for himself. *My relationship with my dad is closer than that of most fathers and sons. Would I trade even some of that to have my mother, faults and all?*

Jake glanced over at Ben, who'd swapped the real world for his computer game. *Ben's not having an easy go of it. He still has both his parents, but they're using him as a weapon in their war against each other.* It seemed the only thing Ben's parents agreed upon was that Ben didn't have the same talent as his prodigy brother, so he needed to work harder. The pressure had reached such a point that Ben would hide out at Jake's house and tell his parents he was at school practicing. Jake didn't mind, as Ben enjoyed cooking and had recently started making dinners at their house—payment for the shelter provided, Ben had joked with his dry wit—which was a nice change from Mr. McGreevy's pizza regimen. *I'm lucky to have a friend like Ben. My life may not be perfect, but whose is?*

Jake decided to keep his theory about his mother to himself. He wasn't sure if he was ready to face facts and decided to wait a bit to let it all sink in. Besides, tomorrow they were performing at the Navy Pier, and he needed to concentrate. Then afterward, he and Julie were planning to exchange Christmas presents.

*　　*　　*

Thursday Morning (Christmas Day, December 25th)

"This should be fun!" Jake commented as he stepped off the bus the next morning.

"Sure, but I wish I didn't have to wear this silly costume."

Julie tugged at her elf outfit. The orchestra was to play a selection of holiday tunes while the gymnasts, dressed as elves, handed out gifts to needy children.

"The kids will love it. It's a great cause," Ben added.

"I know, but I stand out," Julie responded.

Jake smiled. The other gymnasts, all petite, fit the part of elves nicely, while Julie's height made her look out of place. Jake felt a slight tingle as he glanced at Julie with her fake ears and oversized velvet slippers. *Adorable.* His eyes met hers and they both quickly turned away. *Was she looking at me?* A bit more dressed up than usual, he was wearing tuxedo pants, a white shirt, and a bright red cummerbund.

"Well, if it isn't David and his Goliath elf." Samantha's voice penetrated the cold winter air. Jake pressed his lips together. He'd grown a few inches over the summer, but Julie was still taller and he was well aware how they looked together. He often wondered if that's why they had never been a couple. "Take the high road," Jake mumbled, and Julie nodded.

"How about we just cool it for the day, for the sake of the kids?" Julie directed her question at Samantha.

"For the sake of the kids, you should get back on the bus. You'll scare the poor tykes. They'll cry 'mutant elf' and run to their parents, I'm sure." Samantha proceeded toward the entrance of the Crystal Gardens.

Having time to kill before the concert started, most of the gymnasts and musicians sought warmth inside the massive six-story greenhouse. Shaking off the cold, Jake nodded his head in silent appreciation of the architecture. An erector set of steel beams held thousands of glass windows in place, allowing the Chicago winter sun to transform the room into a tropical paradise. Palm trees and flowers of every color adorned the room, and Jake found himself thinking about the island he and his dad had always sailed to. *Someday we'll get back there.*

Water from computerized fountains shot from large potted plants and arced over walkways before splashing down into basins. Jake put his arm out to stop the others. "Ben, Julie," he said.

"On it," they replied in unison.

"What's happening?" Natalie asked.

"Jake's up to something. We're going to keep a watch out," Julie replied. She scanned one side of the room while Ben watched the other. Jake jogged ahead of the students and took his position behind one of the fountains. Like a lion hunting an antelope, he tracked his prey. Jake pulled a nickel from his pocket. Julie and Ben gave a discrete "okay" sign. Jake heard the fountain start to gurgle and quickly jammed the coin into the nozzle, keeping his thumb in place to enable adjustment of the stream. The water sprang from below and he quickly pushed the coin until the jet stream shot in the desired direction.

"Argh!" Samantha's shriek echoed through the massive domed area as the high-pressure cold water drenched her. Jake crawled behind the plants to avoid detection. Samantha stormed off in the direction of the restrooms, the laughter of the crowd following her.

"Nice going," Julie winked.

Jake hid his arm—wet up to his elbow from adjusting the spray—behind his back.

"Jake, maybe you could carry my coat for me?" Natalie offered.

"Perfect." Jake draped her coat over his wet arm to hide it. The smell of Natalie's perfume, which clung to her jacket, gave him a little jolt.

*   *   *

The room for Winter Wonderfest was aglow with lights and energy. A skating rink, indoor roller coasters, and dozens of winter-themed family-friendly activities filled the massive space. Although he was too old for most of the rides, Jake wondered if he could use his lack of height to his advantage and sneak onto a few. The concert was amazing. Each member of the orchestra was alert and focused, the fear of making a mistake in their first public concert driving them to perform their very best. His school in New York had plenty of accomplished musicians, but nothing like this group. Maestro Mancini was crisp with his direction, his eyes seemingly everywhere. With a small glance, he could reward you for a note well played or warn you about an upcoming cue. During a break between songs, Jake watched the elves hand out gifts. The children's twinkling eyes and hopeful faces shined brighter than the halogen lamps lining the nearby wall. *This is a good thing we are doing.* Jake silently vowed not to let another holiday season pass without volunteering at similar events. The toys were inexpensive and by no means spectacular, yet Jake knew these kids would cherish their gifts. *What did I even get last year?* Jake couldn't remember and hoped his father had the receipt for whatever he'd purchased this year so he could return it. *I don't want anything. Wait, I do want something.* The reporter's question still hung in his memory. *Justice for my mother.* Jake's anger over being robbed of a normal childhood—his anger at the selfishness of others—had grown more and more as he absorbed himself in his mother's workbook.

A nudge from Ben brought Jake back to the concert. He rosined his bow and prepared to join in at his assigned time, concentrating on the Maestro and hoping the music would consume his thoughts and calm him. It didn't.

Chapter 19

Thursday Afternoon (December 25th)

Jake quickly changed out of his tuxedo and made his way toward the Stanley House foyer. Julie was standing by the tree waiting for him, right where they had arranged to meet to exchange their gifts. She'd traded her elf costume for a red cardigan sweater and dark green tartan skirt. Jake paused before stepping off the last step. Julie lit up the lobby more than the hundreds of holiday lights. *Simply angelic.*

"Merry Christmas, Jake." Julie gave him a hug.

"Merry Christmas, Jules," Jake replied, his knees quivering a bit. *Chill. She's just your friend.*

"We'd better hurry. The rest of the school will be tramping through here for dinner soon. You first," Julie said, placing a small package into Jake's hands.

"How about we open them at the same time," Jake replied as he handed his gift to Julie.

"Okay."

Jake gently tore at the wrapping, his eyes fixed on Julie and not the task at hand. He watched as she removed the picture frame from the box. Inside the frame was a four-leaf clover mounted on an embroidered doily. A small silver plate at the base of the frame was inscribed with the words "Nothing is luckier than having a friend like you."

"I love it!" Julie exclaimed.

"It's a little corny, I know. But since the clover you found in Ireland was ruined when the bandits captured us, I thought it would be nice to replace it," Jake said.

"It's perfect." Julie leaned in and kissed Jake's cheek. Jake's heart thumped in his chest like the gongs of a grandfather clock.

"Do you like your gift?" Julie asked.

Jake had been so caught up in watching Julie's reaction, he'd barely noticed what was in his hand.

"A belt. I love it." Jake feigned a smile.

"Ha! I was hoping you wouldn't recognize it," Julie beamed.

Jake peered at his gift. "Wait a minute. Is this the Spymaster Special?" Jake pulled slightly on the buckle and a secret compartment popped open. "Awesome! I have a tiny little pen knife that will go perfectly in here." Jake hugged Julie and held on a bit longer than normal.

"Sounds like the others are coming," Julie said. Jake turned around to greet Ben and Natalie.

"Merry Christmas!" they all said to each other.

"Ben, you nailed that solo today, just the way the Maestro thought you would," Jake said.

"Yes, you really sounded great." Natalie complimented Ben.

"Thank you, Natalie. It's easy to sound good next to you," Ben said.

Natalie scrunched her face in confusion.

A spasm of horror crossed Ben's. "Uh, I mean, you bring out the best in me."

Jake stifled a giggle as Ben ping-ponged his accidental insult into a cheese-ball compliment.

"Sweet," Natalie said, reclaiming her usual good humor. Her melted-butter voice matched her soft eyes. Then she asked, "What are you doing with your free day tomorrow?"

Ben's eyes called to Jake for help.

Ben's freezing up again. He must really like Natalie. "We were going to pick the Art Institute day trip." Jake filled the awkward silence.

"Oh, so am I. I would have thought you would go to the aquarium or the Museum of Science and Industry," Natalie replied. "Not that boys don't like art. I didn't mean to stereotype or anything."

"No, it's okay. I want to see the Cassatt mural that my mom was working on before she died." Jake tried to make light of the heavy comment.

Natalie turned pale and her large brown eyes showed genuine concern. "I understand." She reached out to touch his arm.

Jake could sense Ben's discomfort. A potpourri of feelings clouded his mind as his fledgling infatuation with Natalie, loyalty to Ben, and renewed feelings for Julie collided. *Dad's right: Being a teen is tough.*

"Why don't we all go through the museum together?" Jake suggested.

She smiled. "I'd like that."

*　　*　　*

"'It's easy to sound good next to you'? I'm a buffoon," Ben grumbled. Although they'd been back in their room for over two hours, Ben had not yet stopped replaying that humiliating moment with Natalie.

"Take it easy. It wasn't *that* bad—just an accidental slip of the tongue. She said she'd come with us tomorrow, so I'm sure she's not upset or anything," Jake offered.

"She's coming because *you* asked her, not *me*," Ben replied.

Jake silently cursed the situation. He'd felt a resurgence of feelings for Julie when they exchanged gifts, but he was starting to like Natalie, too. *Julie's fantastic—my best friend.*

And Natalie's cute, gadget-oriented, and mature—and she's always thinking ahead. Ugh. What are you feeling, McGreevy? Ben and Jake were very much alike, so it made sense that they were both attracted to Natalie.

"Seems like I'm always overshadowed—by my brother, by you, by everyone," Ben continued.

Jake's chest tightened. He hated it when his friend was down like this. He struggled to find the right words. *Do the right thing: pick your friend over a girl.* "You did sound great today. Natalie was right about that. Plus, she started the conversation with you. I think she likes you."

"Probably just wants me to introduce her to my brother."

The sullen mood in the room was stifling.

"What you need is something sweet to take your mind off Natalie—preferably in the form of that awesome yule log they served today. I saw them box some of it up," Jake said, changing the subject.

"It's past curfew." Ben collapsed on the bed.

"Has that ever stopped us before?"

A spark appeared in Ben's eyes. "Could be dangerous."

"Could be fun," Jake replied.

"We could be expelled."

"Could still be fun." Jake held out his fist.

Ben bumped his knuckles against Jake's.

Chapter 20

Thursday Evening (December 25th)

Jake and Ben, dressed in robes and slippers, headed into the bathroom. Safe from the hallway camera's view, the boys shed their robes, revealing black sweatpants and shirts.

"I can't believe the school has security cameras in every hallway," Ben commented.

"It's not a bad idea these days. Cameras are cheap enough." Jake thought back to his job at the security store. "I noticed the ones in this hallway are wired, but the ones on the main floor and the staircase are newer wireless models."

"I can handle the wireless ones." Ben patted his tablet PC.

"In the event the guard saw us enter the bathroom, he'll be expecting us to return shortly," Jake said. "When we open the door, the light from the bathroom cascading into the dark hallway will temporarily cause the camera to lose focus. I'll help it along by hitting the lens with my Maglite. One hundred and seventy lumens should blind the optics and give us a few seconds to make it to the main staircase. Ready?" Jake flicked his light on.

"One sec." Ben furiously typed away on his PC. "Okay, I just hacked the wireless cameras. Used a routine I found a while back. The security monitor will play the same empty hallway loop for 10 minutes. Any longer and someone might discover the loop."

Jake opened the bathroom door and aimed his flashlight at the camera mounted above the exit as he and Ben sprinted toward it. They hustled down the staircase, the whooshing sound of air left in their wake the only evidence of their movement. The Vibram soles of their dress shoes were perfect for night ops, as the soft material enabled quick steps without the typical clack of shoe on stone.

Jake's pulse raced from the thrill of the mission and the sprint down the two flights. Once on the main floor, he and Ben were at the kitchen door in seconds.

"Time check," he huffed.

"Ninety seconds since the loop started. Plenty of time left. How are you going to get past the lock?" Ben responded.

Jake surveyed the door. "It's a Simplex Unican push-button combo lock. Have to go by human nature and assume it's a pattern more than a number system." Jake tried *1, 5, 2, 4, 3*. The door didn't open. Pressing the tumblers again, he tried another standard pattern of *1, 3, 2, 4*. When he pressed down on the lever handle, the push buttons reset loudly, as if mocking him for his lame attempt.

"Eight minutes left, McGreevy." Ben paced behind Jake.

Dah-dah-dah da ta-da da ta-da, Jake's phone sang. Jake shoved his hand into his pocket to silence the phone, nearly breaking his finger in the process.

"Dean Stanley's coming and we're exposed out here. We'll be expelled!" The stress of Ben's whisper urged Jake to try another combination. Nothing.

"I need a disciplined approach to this." Jake calmly stepped back and scrutinized the door as if he were sizing it up at a hardware store.

"You're cracking jokes about the Dean? Now?" Ben asked.

Jake's eyes rose to the top of the doorway. The room number was stenciled in white on a small black placard: 134.

"Calms me down. Plus the Dean is right: Discipline brings focus, and focus brings success."

Jake stepped forward and pressed the *1* button and then the *3* and *4* simultaneously. Sweeter than any symphony note he'd played, the lock released with a click.

The boys disappeared into the kitchen just as the hallway door opened. Hiding behind the deep fryer, they waited until they no longer heard footsteps.

"Quickly! We have only five minutes left on the camera loop." Ben dragged Jake toward the refrigerator.

It took only moments for the boys to locate the cake and even less time for each of them to scarf down a piece.

"Why can't we just take it with us?" Ben mumbled through chocolate-coated lips.

"Can't have any evidence in our room." Jake swallowed the last bite.

Dashing to the staircase, they began their ascent. Jake's shoes practically blurred in motion as they struck each step. Ben, with his long legs, effortlessly cleared two to three steps at a time. Rounding the corner to the last flight, Ben called out the time: "Seven seconds!"

"Door!" Jake responded.

Ben, who beat Jake to the top, flung the hallway door open. Jake dove through the opening and somersaulted into a kneeling position, aiming his flashlight at the camera. Ben hurdled Jake and crashed through their bedroom doorway, followed moments later by Jake.

Jake landed on top of Ben and was wheezing and laughing when he caught sight of large black shoes on the green carpet.

"Having fun, boys?" Dean Stanley's voice silenced their giggles.

Chapter 21

Thursday Evening (December 25th)

"You have five seconds to explain yourself." The Dean was sitting on the corner of Jake's bed resting his hands on his umbrella. *Ugh! I silenced my phone, so I didn't hear the warning.* Jake mentally kicked himself, although he wasn't sure what he would have done if he had been warned. Jake stared into the man's piercing grey eyes. *He'll see through any story I can fabricate.*

"Sir, we snuck into the kitchen to eat some cake." Jake could hear Ben gulp as the Dean evaluated the response.

"The truth was the best choice. Had it been anything else, some concocted story, I would have sent you home, branded a liar *and* a thief."

"So you're not expelling us?" Ben's voice brimmed with hope.

"No." The man stood up with such speed that Jake believed him to be far more physically fit than he let on.

"You will earn back the cake by helping the kitchen staff prepare breakfast each morning for a week. Report there at 4:00 A.M., starting tomorrow."

"Yes, sir." Jake wasn't sure if he'd rather be expelled or get up every morning well before humans were intended to.

"Plus, you will teach my head of security how you defeated

the cameras and the door lock to ensure that future hooligans like you aren't as successful in their antics."

Ben and Jake nodded as the man exited their room. Jake looked at his friend. A chocolate-covered grin appeared on his face. "It was pretty good cake."

*　　*　　*

Friday Morning (December 26th)

The worst part of kitchen duty was having to get up so early; otherwise they didn't find it too horrible. The staff was friendly and laughed long and hard when Jake retold the story of their escapade. Ben's cooking skills were much appreciated, and Jake kept busy fixing different appliances and performing long-overdue maintenance on the well-used equipment.

"Everything always tastes great, yet the tools back here are borderline junk," Jake commented.

"Yes, well, the Dean prefers to spend money on things more visible than ovens or mixers," one of the staff responded. "Besides, being consistent in quality and detail is artistry itself."

Jake thought back to his mother's comments. *The eyes— the eyes are wrong. Would Cassatt have been consistent in her eyes or would she have changed them?*

"Jake, I need some help here," Ben called.

Jake zigzagged through the bustling kitchen to the bakery section. Ben had his hand in some dough. "What's up?"

"Check the stickiness of this dough. I'm trying to make ciabatta to serve with the soup tonight, but I messed up the proportions." Ben tried to pull his hands out of the dough, but they were stuck like a pointer in a Chinese finger trap.

"Dude, I thought you knew your way around a kitchen. How could this happen?" Jake snickered.

"I cook. I don't bake, which is why I wanted to try to make the bread—to learn. Now go get some wax paper and flour."

Jake returned and spent nearly ten minutes unsticking his friend's hands from the dough. The head cook threw the whole pan out instead of messing with the dough himself. "Try not to do that again," he huffed.

"Yes, sir. I remember what I did wrong, so it won't happen again," Ben called needlessly to the retreating form of the cook.

"Let's go. I told Julie last night we'd meet by the school crest in the main hall before the bus ride to the Art Institute." Jake nodded in the direction of the door.

*   *   *

Julie frowned when Jake told her the story of the late-night chocolate cake excursion. "You realize that if you get expelled, I'll be here all alone."

"I'm sorry. We were just having a little adventure. I wasn't thinking."

"It's okay. But please behave yourself from now on. New Year's would be really depressing without you." Julie walked outside, trailed by Jake, Ben, and Natalie. They boarded the bus and others chatted away as they wound their way through the Chicago streets, but Jake remained silent. Thoughts of Natalie, Julie, his recent run-in with the Dean, and the music camp flowed through his mind like a rushing river. But a boulder disrupting the water's flow was the thought of his mother's death. No matter how busy he kept his mind, he kept returning to her and her final days. *She must have known she was in danger. Why else would she stash the notebook and hide that message inside the bear?*

The bus lurched to a stop and Jake disembarked with the rest of the students. Built of large stone blocks, the Art Institute of Chicago housed more than three hundred thousand works of art and historic artifacts. From the marble floors of the lobby rose massive pillars that supported a gilded wood-paneled ceiling. The kids entered the grand foyer and twirled around, taking in the majestic columns and elaborate design. Jake stopped and stared at the wall near the second-floor exhibits.

"Look! It's the Potter Palmer and Bertha Honoré Palmer Gallery." Jake's pulse raced.

"You know them?" Natalie asked.

"I read about them. The Palmers were heavily involved in the art community in the late nineteenth century. Bertha was the one who hired Mary Cassatt to do the mural."

"Not sure I've ever seen you this excited about art patrons," Ben commented.

"I know. Punch me later for my geekiness, but something about seeing their names makes my mom's notebook more real. She wrote about them and studied them, and here they have an entire gallery in their names. They existed, and therefore my mom existed . . ." Jake's voice trailed off.

"I get it. It's like connecting puzzle pieces. You think, 'No way this pile of debris makes a picture,' but bit by bit you can see the scene form," Natalie said.

Jake smiled at her. "Exactly."

*   *   *

Jake and Julie hung back, allowing Ben and Natalie to walk by themselves through the museum exhibits. Despite residual feelings of jealousy and regret, Jake was glad that Natalie seemed focused on Ben. Ben motioned to something and spoke to Natalie. She looked aghast and suddenly Ben's face turned crimson.

"Guess he made a joke and it backfired. It's a bit like watching a Little League game: kids trying their best but also committing a lot of errors," Julie commented.

"Good analogy," Jake replied. He could see Julie was struggling to say something, so he remained quiet for a few minutes.

"Zach and I broke up last night," she said.

"Again?" Jake blurted out. "I mean, I—"

"That's okay. I know what you meant. It *has* been a few times—five, I think. But this one may stick."

"Why?"

"This time we both agreed. Our other breakups were after big fights and were more of an emotional reaction. Last night we decided that our schedules and goals were too far apart to make it really work. He's even talking of transferring to another school with a better football team," Julie said.

"I'm sorry to hear that." *Am I?* Jake stopped in front of the massive Cassatt mural. "I've never really had as long a relationship as you and Zach have had, so I can't relate to your feelings. But we're only in high school. No real rush."

"I know. Breaking up shouldn't be a big deal. But I'm still disappointed and sad," Julie replied.

Jake reached out to hold her hand. His heart skipped when she didn't pull away and instead interlaced their fingers. *What are we doing?*

"This was the mural she was reviewing when she died." Jake gazed up at the massive painting.

"It's really beautiful."

Jake bobbed his head in agreement, processing his mother's description of it. The damaged area had been repaired, so only slight blemishes remained. He walked closer and peered into the cold eyes of the woman reaching up for the fruit.

"Mr. McGreevy?" a man's voice called. Jake turned to see a tall bald man approaching them. A petite woman walked swiftly beside him.

"Yes?" Jake unconsciously stepped closer to Julie.

"Conner Royal, museum director. And this is Annica Taylor, head of Impressionist and Postmodern Art."

"From the notebook," Jake blurted.

Chapter 22

Friday Morning (December 26th)

"Excuse me?" Conner asked.

"Sorry. Nice to meet you. Is something wrong?"

"Nothing. Nothing at all. I saw you on the news the other night, so I called Stanley House and they told me you were coming here today. I had the security guards keep an eye out for you. I wanted to meet you, to meet Karen's son." Conner offered his hand. Jake and Julie shook hands with both Annica and Conner.

"You recognized me from the news?"

"Yes. I want you to know that your mother was a very remarkable and memorable person."

Jake caught a note of sadness in the man's voice. "Thank you. I wish I had known her myself."

"She talked of you often. For the couple of days that I accompanied her while she studied the mural, she was always speaking either about art or you," Annica added.

Jake blushed. "So this is the painting she was working on?"

"Our pride and joy. More than any other single piece of art here, this work draws in the most people—the mystery behind its disappearance combined with the sheer size of it . . ." The director reached his hand out and placed it on

Jake's shoulder. "I'm very sorry about your mother. I truly am. Please let us know if there is anything we can do to make your stay in Chicago more enjoyable."

Jake nodded and shook the man's hand again before the director and Annica excused themselves. When they disappeared around the corner, Julie said, "Wow, your mom must have made quite an impression if they wanted to meet you after all these years."

"I suppose so," Jake answered distractedly. "Come on, Julie—let's catch up with the others." Gripping her arm at the elbow, he quickly steered for the exit. The surprise of meeting someone listed in his mom's binder had spiked his blood pressure.

After meeting up with Ben and Natalie, Jake and Julie merged into a line with the rest of the students and boarded the bus. Jake plopped into his seat and leaned his head against the window. Something caught his eye lurking by the lion's head: a man with a horrible fake tan and overly black hair. Jake's heart pounded.

"Jake? You look as if you just saw a ghost," Ben said.

"Worse. I think I just saw my mother's killer."

Chapter 23

Friday Evening (December 26th)

After a quiet but uneasy bus ride back to Stanley House, the gang gathered in the far corner of the dining hall. After a few minutes, Natalie excused herself, as she had a scheduled evening session with the Maestro. She hated to tear herself away, but Jake understood. With his own private meeting scheduled for the following night, Jake's fear of playing alone for the man was never far from his thoughts. He wished Natalie luck.

Jake pulled out the tattered pages from his mom's notebook. Fanning them out, he explained his theory that the Cassatt hanging in the Art Institute was a fake and that Bronzer was behind his mom's death. When he finished talking, he felt as if he'd just run a marathon in blazing heat.

Scanning the pages with Ben and Julie, Jake pointed out the various notes his mom had written about the people she'd interviewed over the years, and about the reviews she'd conducted of old letters and documents pertaining to the missing Cassatt. "Look here. She wrote two theories as to the mural's whereabouts on this page." Jake held up one of the last pages.

My theories:

1: Many articles and paintings from the 1893 World's Fair were subsequently stored in the Palace of Fine Arts. Looking at old blueprints, I see there is an anterior room at the end of the west hall on the main level. Based on construction records, this room was sealed during the renovation prior to its 1933 reopening as the Museum of Science and Industry. I can find no mention of the room's discovery in any newspaper. It is conceivable the mural is still in that room.

2: Michael Reese Hospital. Built in 1907, this hospital was the finest medical institution at the time. One of the architects, Richard Schmidt, apprenticed with Henry Cobb, who built the Palmer Hotel. In 1907, Bertha corresponded with Schmidt about hanging the mural in the Michael Reese Hospital on the south side of Chicago. It's possible the mural made it there but was simply never hung.

"So your mom came up with these theories, but before she could explore them, someone staged the discovery of the mural," Julie said. Tears formed in her eyes and Ben's face lost all its color.

"So what should we do? Go to the police?" Julie asked.

"With what? The shiftiness of a man with orange skin?" Ben answered the question for Jake.

"I agree with Ben, although I wouldn't have put it that tersely." Jake elbowed his friend. "I think we should check out the two places my mom thought held the original Cassatt. If we can find it, the police will have to reopen the case," Jake stated.

"Correction. We'll check out the first place. I just read on my computer that the Michael Reese Hospital was demolished in 2009. If your mom was right about that place, then the real mural would have been discovered around then, because, most likely, everything important would have been removed from the building before it was bulldozed," Ben stated.

"Ugh. We can't catch a break," Jake moaned. "Okay, we'll search the Palace of Fine Arts and hope for the best," Jake said.

"I'm in. It will be great to focus on something important—and to take my mind off gymnastics." Julie let her head slump to the table. "*È così difficile per me.*" This time, she didn't need to translate. Everyone knew how she was feeling, even if they didn't understand all the words.

"It can't be that bad," Jake said.

"I can't perform the simple maneuver of tossing my stick into the air, catching the end of the ribbon, and flicking it so that the stick flies back into my hand."

"Oh, yeah, that's really simple. I think I mastered that, like, in kindergarten," Jake joked.

Julie lifted her head up and glared at him. He could tell she was trying to hold back a smile, so he engaged her in a staring contest. They both laughed at the same time. As Jake looked at her, he realized his crush on her was officially back. *Chill, Jake. You're just rebounding because Natalie showed more interest in Ben.*

"What does your coach say?" Ben asked.

"He said that with a bit of confidence and more practice, I'll not only master it, I'll move to the next level."

"Sounds like a smart guy. He probably sees the same determination that I saw in you when you were swinging in the Irish cave. He knows you'll be awesome," Jake said.

Julie gave him a smile and took a sip from her drink. "So where exactly is this palace?"

"It's the Museum of Science and Industry now. It used to be the Palace of Fine Arts back during the World's Fair. We can go to the retirement home, play some music for a bit, and then take a cab over to the museum. It's only a few miles away, so it won't take long." Jake laid his beaten-up guide-book on the table. The others crowded around him.

"Cool. Maybe we'll have time to swing by the submarine. The guys that went there today said it was pretty awesome. I'm sure it's better than the Art Institute," Ben lamented.

"So you would have chosen a submarine tour over hanging out with Natalie?" Julie teased.

"That's my boy, Ben! Forget spending the day with a beautiful and smart musician. Give him a rusty tub of metal and the smell of seventy-year-old grease," Jake piled on.

"Very funny." Ben blushed and then brightened. "If she comes tomorrow, then I'll get both. I'll go wait outside the music room to ask her."

*   *   *

Saturday Morning (December 27th)

Jake and Ben were beginning to enjoy kitchen duty—and they never had to pilfer a sweet treat again. After another intense morning of practice, the kids piled into the van for the now-familiar trip to the retirement home after lunch. When they arrived, Jake pulled Natalie aside. "Ben told you we were going to skip over to the Museum of Science and Industry, right?"

"Yes. He told me all about your mother and what you're trying to do."

"And you know we could be sent home or given extra chores for this?"

"I know. I still want to go. A lot of people think I'm this goody two-shoes, but I *can* be wild. In fact, this one time, I was supposed to lead Tchaikovsky's *Violin Concerto in D Major*, but I was angry with the conductor, so I started playing Vivaldi's *Four Seasons* instead. The orchestra had no choice but to follow my lead!" Natalie exclaimed, her voice squeaking.

"A real rebel. We'll have to keep an eye on you." Jake grinned.

Hannah rushed over when the kids entered the lobby and she quickly organized a group of residents to listen to the three violinists perform. The tile floor acted like a natural amplifier and the sound echoed through the hallways, enticing even more residents out of their rooms. Soon they had nearly fifty people in the audience. The weavers stopped working on their latest projects, and even the VFW came over to listen. In between songs, Julie performed her gymnastic maneuvers.

"One more song and then we need to bolt if we're going to make it to the museum and back," Jake said.

"Oh, let's do 'Jingle Bells,' but in a rockabilly style like Brian Setzer. Ben, you can lead off," said Natalie, her eyes radiating hope and excitement. Jake could almost hear Ben's silent scream.

"You sure we should do that? It's a pretty fast tempo and we wouldn't want anyone here to throw out a hip or something." Jake's attempt to save his friend fell on deaf ears as Natalie continued to stare at Ben.

Ben straightened his posture—physical evidence of the confidence growing inside him. "Let's rock this house," Ben shouted with a mix of bravado and true courage.

His first note was wrong, but the fast tempo didn't allow for any self-reflection and he quickly found his groove. Twenty seconds in and the fire from Ben's violin spoke to his true talent. Jake and Natalie joined in, as Julie attempted to accompany them on a makeshift percussion set of utensils and plastic cafeteria trays. Several of the seniors stood up and started swing dancing.

Hannah clapped along, grinning joyfully. "My goodness, I haven't had my heart beat like this since I met Nat King Cole," she exclaimed after they finished.

The crowd enveloped the kids, expressing their delight and relating stories about their glory days on the dance floor. By the time the kids broke free, they were well behind schedule. The home's driver agreed to run them over to the museum, saving them the time it would have taken to hail a cab.

Chapter 24

Saturday Afternoon (December 27th)

"We're about thirty minutes behind schedule," Jake called as he rushed up the stone steps and through the entry doors. They purchased tickets and then used the escalator to reach the main level.

"Wow." Jake absent-mindedly stopped at the top of the escalator to gaze at the sight ahead of them, causing Ben to ram into him.

"Focus, man. Focus!" Ben yelped.

"What—oh, sorry, Ben!" Jake picked up the pace.

"Lackluster discipline, my friend—mighty disappointing," Ben grumbled.

Ignoring his friend's joke, Jake walked a few feet into the rotunda. Neon blue light cascaded through the massive open space. Three wings jutted off the entryway. Each acted like a siren calling Jake—and any other fan of all things cool—to come explore.

"I was wrong. I would trade a pretty girl for this," Jake said.

"What was that?" Natalie asked.

Julie stepped behind Jake and thumped his shoulder with her museum map. "Jake was just commenting how glad he is that we're here—to look for the mural, may I remind us all?"

"Right." Jake kept walking on autopilot, taking it all in. The east wing displayed various forms of transportation, from a large locomotive and a commercial airliner to World War II planes. A piece of massive industrial equipment adorned the entrance to the southern hall. Jake knew from his guidebook that it was part of one of the original exhibits, a mock-up of a coal mine.

"Check out that coal mine. We should go down into it," Ben said.

Jake and Julie exchanged a knowing glance. "We'll pass, thank you."

"Oh, yeah. I forgot you guys were trapped underground in Ireland," Ben replied.

"This way." Jake pointed toward the west wing, devoted to the science of storms. They walked by crowds of people and past interesting exhibits, including a tsunami machine, an avalanche demonstration, and a fire chamber. Suspended from the ceiling, a twenty-foot Tesla coil belched controlled bolts of lightning to a surrounding metal ring. Members of the largest crowd waited their turn to stand in the middle of a forty-foot-high manmade tornado.

They reached the western edge of the exhibit and stopped at a door that read "Staff Members Only."

"If there is a hidden room, it's back there. Why don't I go alone? That way if I get caught, only I will get into trouble," Jake said.

"We're in this together, Jake." Julie went to push the door open.

"I think Jake's right. Not that I'm afraid to get caught, but one person roving around back there is far less noticeable than four," Ben said.

"You guys go see the museum. I'll meet you back at the escalators in twenty minutes." Jake swiveled his head around. Satisfied nobody was watching, he disappeared through the door. The secluded hallway, in stark contrast to the exhibition area, was conspicuously quiet. Jake strode through the maze of dull eggshell-white walls and plain speckled tile. Several storage rooms branched off the hallway into which Jake cautiously stuck his head. Each time, he found no sign of another room, not that he really knew what that sign would be. Arriving at an emergency exit, he paused. *Come on. It has to be here.*

"Are you lost, son?" a low voice called from behind him. Jake turned to see an elderly man dressed in a custodian's uniform. "Walter" was embroidered on the left chest pocket.

Jake had planned for just such an event. "Maybe. I'm writing a history paper for school and in one old book, I learned of a hidden room, the most western in the building, that might have housed some works of art a long time ago."

Walter crossed his arms and rested his chin in his hand. "Let me think. It seems to me that back in the seventies they renovated this part of the building. They did find a room that had been walled off. Yes, I remember it. It was the year my son was born and I had just started here. Everyone was really excited because there were some small artifacts from the 1800s in it."

"Small?" Jake's heart tightened.

"Yes, some vases and such. Nothing really came of it, if I recall. Does that help?"

Rats. A dead end. "Ah . . . yeah. Thanks."

Walter escorted Jake back to the public exhibit area. Jake thanked the man for his time, shoved his hands into his pockets, and sulked toward the entranceway.

Brooding about his rotten luck, he suddenly felt a choking sensation as a strong hand grasped the back collar of his jacket and twisted it tight.

"Keep quiet and walk normal," a rough voice whispered.

Jake glanced over his shoulder at the orange face behind him. *Bronzer!*

"Let go of me!" Jake wheezed, as the man steered him through the crowds.

"Shut up. Another word and I'll squeeze harder." For emphasis the man wrapped his large fingers around Jake's neck, further restricting his air supply.

Fear enveloped Jake. Pulse pounding, he fought the urge to scream or run. *Focus, McGreevy.* As he walked under the 1.2-million-volt ceiling-mounted Tesla coil, his fingers, still stuffed inside his coat pocket, wrapped around some loose change. Praying his timing was right, he flicked his wrist and launched the money skyward. With a buzz, the coil energized and lightning bolts shot from the center sphere. The electricity struck the coins and sparks cascaded to the floor. Nearby patrons screamed in shock and confusion as they rushed away from the lightning exhibit. Jake felt the grip on his neck loosen and, without looking back, he tore free from the goon and vaulted over a toddler on his way to the exit. As he neared the center area, he saw another man, dressed in weathered jeans and a frayed bomber jacket, charging at him. *Bronzer has friends!* Dodging left, Jake flew up the stairs to the museum's balcony level.

"Get him!"

Jake heard the angry voice followed by the noise of feet thundering up the stairs behind him. Never slowing, Jake clutched the smooth wood banister, sprang over the railing, and landed on the wing of the Boeing 727 suspended high above the gallery floor.

CLANG! CLANG! CLANG!

Jake ignored the loud ringing of the fire alarm as he jumped onto the waiting wing of the nearby Spitfire World War II airplane. Using a baseball-style slide, he hurtled down and landed on top of a large black locomotive. A quick descent down the train engine's ladder and he was on the main floor again, merging with the throngs of museum-goers who were evacuating to the sound of the fire alarm. Jake started to breathe a little easier as an ocean of people now separated him from the thugs.

"Jake, over here!" Julie's voice rang above the noise of the crowd as he scrambled down the main steps outside the museum. Like a lighthouse beckoning a ship on a stormy sea, her shining face guided him to the safety of a waiting taxi. He wedged himself into the backseat with Julie and Natalie.

"Go, go, go!" Ben instructed the driver from the front passenger seat. The cab jumped from the curb, nearly hitting a man trying to videotape the museum's evacuation with his cell phone.

Jake craned his neck to watch the museum disappear into the background. "What just happened there?" He coughed as he spoke, his throat and chest tightening both from his race through the transportation gallery and the chokehold he'd endured.

"We heard the commotion and saw that man chasing you," Julie said.

"Then Natalie sent me to hold a cab while she pulled the fire alarm so you could blend in with the masses. Quick thinking, huh?" Ben's voice pulsed with pride.

Jake turned to Natalie, who was blushing. "Nice going. You'll fit right in."

Chapter 25

Saturday Afternoon (December 27th)

The gang made it back to Hannah's with just enough time to gather their instruments and enjoy another cup of her special blend before the Stanley House shuttle arrived. Sitting in the back and talking in hushed tones, they decided that there was safety in numbers and agreed that Jake would never go anywhere without at least one of them with him. They had debated calling the police but chose not to when they realized they could be sent home for violating the rules of Stanley House, which would mean they would lose any chance of finding the real Cassatt or bringing Jake's mom's murderer to justice. Exhausted and shaken after their excursion, they ate dinner with little discussion. After saying good night, Jake headed for his room, where he knew Mr. Sandman would not be waiting for him with sleep. The events of the day had him wound up, and even if Jake thought he might nap, Ben was so jazzed by Natalie, he couldn't stop talking.

"And get this, Jake. She goes to school on the other side of Manhattan, *but* she lives only eight blocks from where I do," Ben prattled on.

Jake tried to grunt in the appropriate places so as not to be rude. He was glad for Ben, but it was early to be head over heels. *Of course, I'm feeling a little twitterpated with Julie . . . again.* The entire ride home, Julie hadn't let go of Jake's arm and kept saying how glad she was that he was safe. Jake chuckled.

"What's so funny?" Ben asked.

"We are. I had a guy grab me today and you're droning on about Natalie and I'm . . ." Jake stopped himself. He rarely discussed his feelings with anyone.

"What, Jake? I'm pouring myself out here and you always just clam up. It's Julie, right?"

Jake nodded. "Yes, and that's what's funny. Despite all that's happening, I keep thinking about her."

"Teenage hormones, my friend," Ben snorted. "My mom pretty much blames everything I do on them!"

"I wish I could put them on hold right now so I could focus," Jake said.

"There is a lot going on. Julie, Natalie, the art mystery, your mom. Add that to the challenges of this performing arts camp and we've got a busy holiday season," Ben added.

The camp. "The Maestro!" Jake eyed his watch. "I'm going to be late to my private session!" He grabbed his violin and tore from the room.

*   *   *

Bursting into the hall and tripping over a music stand, Jake sprawled to the floor, his violin sliding and stopping at the feet of the Maestro.

"Sorry I'm late," Jake groaned.

"Quite all right, Jake. A good musician always makes a bold entrance, and it seems you've mastered that." Maestro Mancini's calm voice helped soothe Jake's nerves.

The conductor waited patiently while Jake stood up, retrieved his violin, and prepared to play.

"What would you like me to start with?" Jake asked.

"Nothing specific. I'm just going to hum and you're going to follow as quickly as you can."

"What song?" Jake peered at his teacher.

"I'm going to make it up as I go."

"I don't understand. How can I follow along if I don't know the song or have any music?" Jake lowered his violin.

The Maestro reached up to tug his earlobe. "We have these for a reason. They're a musician's greatest gift. You'll listen and then play a note that most closely resembles my pitch."

You gotta be kidding me. I'm stressing out here and he's getting all Mr. Miyagi on me. Jake gulped. "Okay."

The man hummed one long note. Jake guessed a C sharp and drew his bow across the strings. A quick nod of approval from the Maestro allowed Jake to breathe a bit. The man increased the pace of the notes and Jake struggled to keep up. After ten grueling minutes, Jake's shirt was drenched in sweat. Never before had he perspired as much as he had at this camp.

"Good," Maestro Mancini said. "That was the best yet— best of all the students here. I can tell you're a quick thinker, someone used to handling pressure situations."

"Thank you."

"But I can also tell you're clouded. You aren't freeing your mind the way you should. What's troubling you?" The man's comforting gaze melted some of Jake's interior walls.

"My mom."

"Ah, yes. I saw the news crew here. She died when you were very young, right?"

"Yes, sir. I was two years old, so I don't really have any memories of her. But being here in Chicago, where she died . . ." Jake's voice trailed off.

"My father died of cancer when I was five. I have a few memories, images and feelings mostly." The Maestro looked off to his left, trying to remember. "It's not fair, not knowing them, is it? I don't think it really affected me until my teens. Everyone handles these types of things differently. For me, it was reckless behavior. Stealing cars, vandalism, fights. I was out of control."

"That seems very hard to believe," Jake said.

Maestro Mancini smiled. "Just imagine the energy I put into conducting. Now imagine that energy with nothing positive to focus it on."

"Fireworks," Jake nodded.

"Exactly. I was quite the lout, lacking focus and discipline, as the Dean would say." They both chuckled.

"So what happened?" Jake leaned forward in his seat.

"My mother finally found a way to reach me. She had all of our family and friends, anyone who knew my father, write down short stories and memories of him and then put them all in a box. When I was feeling angry or sad, she would pull out a memory and make me read it. Through their eyes, I learned who my father was. I learned he loved music, so I picked up a violin and started playing."

"And now you're the best," Jake said.

"No, not the best, but good enough that I get to teach the best." He winked at Jake.

*   *   *

Jake let the steam from the hot shower soak into his pores. After his private session, he wanted some alone time, and within the walls of the crowded and busy school, the shower was the only real escape. He liked Mancini's idea about the memory box. He could probably set up a website and let anyone who knew his mom post memories—people like the Art Museum director, who had obviously remembered her. Jake reached for the faucet handles and then stopped. *Not yet. I need another minute or two to think.*

114

Two more minutes turned into ten and Jake's skin wrinkled like a prune's.

"Thought I was going to have to send a search-and-rescue team in after you," Ben kidded when Jake returned to the room.

"Thinking through some things."

"Solve anything?"

"Of course not."

"Yeah. That dumb showerhead never seems to tell you what to do," Ben said with a tone that spoke to the numerous times he'd been deep in thought.

I've been so self-absorbed, I haven't asked about Ben's parents' divorce. "How are things with your parents?"

"There isn't much new. My dad sent a text today saying they've nearly worked out a custody arrangement. Crazy, right—arguing over who gets me, as if I'm some sort of property?"

"Did they ever ask you what you wanted?" Jake asked.

"No. But that's fine with me. I don't know which one I would choose. I mean, how do you pick a parent?" Ben turned to his computer and then swiveled back around. "I'm sorry, Jake. That wasn't cool. You didn't even get that option."

"That's okay, bro," Jake smiled. "I caught a bad break early, but since then, I've been pretty lucky."

Ben nodded before returning to his game.

Chapter 26

Sunday Morning (December 28th)

"We're going to do a little switch here this morning," Maestro Mancini said, motioning for Jake, Ben, and Natalie to stand up. "Ben, you're taking first chair. Natalie will move to second, and Jake will round out our excellent violin section in third."

Jake grinned as he saw all the blood drain from Ben's face.

"Sir, that's not right. They're *both* better than I am. This isn't right," Ben stuttered.

"Ben, he *is* right. You're the best. Don't worry about Jake and me. Maestro Mancini talked about it with us before and we're totally okay with this," Natalie interjected.

Ben looked at Jake, pleading with his eyes.

"She speaks the truth. You are now the Jedi Master." Jake caught a glimpse of excitement on Ben's face before fear pushed it away.

This was the first dress rehearsal: the rhythmic gymnasts would be performing with the orchestra in the large auditorium. For the concert at the Navy Pier, the musicians had played while the athletes handed out gifts and taught the kids how to twirl ribbons. This time they would actually be performing to the music. Maestro Mancini floated through the orchestra talking with the students—reminding some of key areas to pay attention to and complimenting others. Jake admired him for his quiet yet firm style of leadership, mixing equal parts motivator and educator.

As best he could, Jake searched for Julie out of the corners of his eyes. *She's somewhere in the wings, waiting. I hope she nails this.* They started playing, and Jake immediately noticed a change in Ben's string work: crisp, precise. *Good for Ben.* He and Natalie winked at each other. Suddenly the room was alive with motion as colorful lights flashed all around and gymnasts flooded the stage, performing intricately timed cartwheels and dance moves. Jake doubled his focus on the Maestro, having underestimated the difficulty of playing music with the distraction of teenage girls flipping end over end in front of him.

He found his groove and was able to sneak an occasional peek at Julie. She seemed to be doing well, but Jake's ability to spot sloppy maneuvers was poor. *And here we go.* The orchestra struck up "O Christmas Tree," the big finale, where the athletes simulated decorating a Christmas tree. Julie's role required her to snake her ribbon around as if it were tinsel wrapping the tree. She glided across the stage and moved her arm in a giant arc. As the stick reached its apogee, though, the ribbon flew from Julie's hand and landed in the percussion section of the orchestra.

CRASH!

The sound of symbols being knocked from their stands echoed throughout the room, followed by sporadic laughter. *Oh, no!* Jake's stomach twisted. Julie bolted from the room, her hands attempting to cover her face.

Jake looked up at the conductor. The Maestro gave him a brisk nod of approval. Jake dropped his violin onto his chair and chased after Julie. *Man, she's fast.* Julie wouldn't stop despite Jake's calls. She hit the emergency exit door and skidded to a halt in the desolate snow-covered field in the back of the school.

Head down and crying, Julie's body quivered.

Jake stood there for a moment, unsure of how to even comfort her. He reached to touch her arm, paused, and then lowered his. In all their years together, he had never seen her this upset.

He shivered as the harsh wind sliced into his skin. Glancing down, he realized Julie was standing in the snow in her bare feet. "You need to go inside before you get frostbite!"

"Perfect. Then I can leave here," Julie sobbed.

Jake clenched his fists in frustration. *What do I say?* "These things happen. I mean, it's only our first rehearsal."

"I don't understand what went wrong. I executed it flawlessly in warm-ups. The stick just flew out of my hand. I can't go back in there. Do you know how embarrassing that is?" Julie's voice cracked with frustration.

Jake started to respond but thought better of it. Truth be told, he had no idea how that felt and knew if he tried to sympathize, she'd see right through it. "I don't know how that feels. I do know you're the strongest and most driven girl I've ever met." Jake took a step forward and grasped both of her arms with his hands. She shrugged his hands off and instead wrapped her arms around him.

"Oh, Jake, I just wanted to show Samantha I could do it. Argh!"

Her warmth felt good in the freezing temperature. "Maybe it shouldn't be about beating her."

"I know. But she's just been so horrible to me." Julie let go of Jake but didn't step away.

Her eyes locked with his and he felt an incredible force pushing him toward her. Stretching up, he leaned in and gave her a quick kiss on the cheek. "It will be okay. Now let's go inside while you still have feet."

She continued to stare at him, and he felt awkward and thrilled at the same time.

"Okay," she nodded.

With the emergency doors locked, Jake and Julie had to navigate around the massive building to the front entrance. Jake offered to give Julie a piggyback ride, but to save him the embarrassment of not being able to carry her, she opted to take his socks instead. The wool blend offered enough protection for her to make it around the building without any permanent damage. The security guard by the front door gave them a stern look before smiling. Jake—with his sockless dress shoes—and Julie—in a leotard and black dress socks—made quite a pair. Once inside, Julie headed for her room to shower and change, while Jake ran to his room for another pair of socks before making his way to lunch. He replayed the morning's events in his mind again. Had he said the right things? Should he have given her that kiss? Although the gesture was like something a friend would do to comfort a friend, he had never kissed her before, even on the cheek.

"Is Julie okay?" Ben asked when Jake sat down at their usual table.

"I think she *will* be. I feel so bad for her," Jake responded.

"Yeah, I saw it fly from her hand. It reminded me of a quarterback losing control of a wet football." Ben gulped his iced tea.

Jake dropped his fork. "I'm going to go check something out. Can you take my tray back?"

"Sure," Ben replied, but Jake was already headed for the door.

Jake ran through the hallway and back into the concert hall. He rooted around the percussion equipment section. Not finding what he was looking for there, Jake searched under a stack of chairs in the far corner and spotted the wayward ribbon stick. *Just as I thought.* The grip tape normally affixed to the handle was missing. After searching near the stage, Jake found the pieces of grip tape. A slippery substance was coated on the inside of the tape. *Someone removed the original tape and replaced it with this tape. But instead of glue, it was attached with this grease, so when Julie swung her arm, the stick slid free of the tape.*

"Samantha," Jake growled. He spun around and ran through the halls until he reached the administrative section. It didn't take him long to find the door he was seeking.

Chapter 27

Sunday Evening (December 28th)

"I . . . I think I missed a few notes," Ben said.

"Cut it out. You were perfect. I know you're just trying to be humble, but it's okay to be happy every once in a while when you do well." Jake took a bite of meatloaf. The four friends were gathered at dinner, each having spent the afternoon alone practicing.

"Any more issues with your game, Ben?" Jake asked.

"None. In fact, I have a new ally." Ben winked at Natalie.

"Natalie's playing?" Jake raised an eyebrow.

"She was the one pranking me. I finally figured it out when I saw the other player was only online at the same times as I was. It had to be someone here." Ben grinned.

"I saw Ben playing the game on the bus and decided to have some fun. I told you! I can have a wild side," Natalie said.

"How did you figure out his user name?" Jake was impressed once again by her.

"I scanned through the list of players and saw *Anything-but-piano* and figured that had to be Ben's wry humor."

"I guess my rivalry with my brother is a bit too obvious," Ben said.

The mood changed from jovial to serious, causing Jake to search for a subject change.

He spotted a bandage on Julie's hand. "Did you give yourself blisters practicing?"

Julie blushed. "You know me too well. I just can't let it beat me."

"I can assure you with a high degree of certainty that it won't happen again. It wasn't your fault," Jake said, grinning.

"What do you mean?" Julie replied.

"Someone messed with—" The crackle of the public address system cut Jake off.

"Samantha Rigby, Julie O'Brien, and Jake McGreevy. Please report to the Dean's office," a stern voice called over the speaker.

Julie's face contorted in confusion.

"Come on." Jake grabbed her hand.

*   *   *

Julie fidgeted with her shirt while Samantha twirled her hair, both trying to expel their nervous energy. Jake did his best not to look smug.

"I understand there is an ongoing quarrel between you girls," the Dean said, entering his office.

Samantha tried to look innocent. "No, sir. We just—"

"Enough. I'm not falling for that. You think you're the first person to try to outsmart me? This isn't a game, young lady," the Dean barked.

Jake bit down hard on his tongue to keep from laughing.

"I don't know who started it or why it continues, but I'm disappointed it was brought into my school. I can put up with a few petty disagreements, but you've crossed the line now, Ms. Rigby. Mr. McGreevy brought some security footage to my attention." The Dean turned his computer screen around to show a recording from the concert hall's left wing. Gymnasts were running back and forth onto the stage. Off to the side, highlighted by the security department, was the image of Samantha pulling a ribbon stick from a duffle bag instead of from the equipment rack and carrying it toward the stage. The camera footage switched perspective to the stage, showing Samantha as she handed the ribbon stick to Julie.

"You sabotaged me?" Julie glared at Samantha.

"I . . . I can explain," Samantha stammered.

"Don't bother. Altering gym equipment jeopardized the safety of all the students. You are herewith expelled and an airport shuttle bus is on its way to get you. One of the staff members will escort you back to New York."

Jake held back a cheer.

Fear and shock broke out all over Samantha's face.

Probably the first genuine emotion I've seen her have.

"Sir," Julie said meekly.

"Yes, Ms. O'Brien." The Dean, still fired up, turned toward her.

"I'm no fan of Samantha's, and yesterday, I would have loved to see her leave. But she is a good gymnast and we need her for the performance. For the sake of the charities, I ask if you would reconsider your decision." When the Dean didn't answer right away, Julie added, "After all, this is the season of forgiveness, isn't it?" Julie said.

Wow, Jake thought.

The Dean's eyes twinkled as he pondered the suggestion. "That is most generous of you, Julie. I may have misjudged you." The Dean extended his hand for Julie to shake. "All right."

"All right?" Samantha squeaked. "I can stay?"

"Yes. But you will wash dishes after each meal for the rest of the time you are here. And you will assist the janitorial staff in cleaning the women's restrooms each night. That should keep you busy enough so that you don't get any more dangerous ideas."

123

Jake heard Samantha suck in a deep breath and wondered if she was regretting the Dean's change of heart. As they left the office, Julie discretely squeezed Jake's hand in a silent thank you.

*   *   *

Perfect. Jake entered the library and found it deserted, as he had expected. He padded through the aisles hoping to find a section on Chicago history. After leaving the Dean's office, Samantha and Julie went back to the dining hall to talk, hoping to improve their relationship over dessert. Ben was back at his game, this time working *with* Natalie.

Something about the Palmers and the Cassatt gnawed at Jake. Internet searches proved to be fruitless. Finding the sections he was searching for, Jake loaded up on every book dealing with Chicago or art history. *Sometimes it's just impossible to connect the dots on a ten-inch screen.* Several titles seemed promising: *The Men and Women Who Built Chicago, Turn-of-the-Century Chicago,* and *The 1893 World's Fair.* The library hadn't been updated in quite some time, but since the subject he was researching was more than 100 years old, Jake figured that that was okay. He dropped the books onto a large oak table and then pulled the chain on a tall desk lamp to help illuminate his work area. At first, Jake was fascinated with the history of the city and read every page. Each time he would find something of interest, he put a yellow sticky on the page from the pad he'd borrowed from the office. He was intrigued to learn how Chicago became known as the Windy City. He'd always assumed it was due to the strong winds coming from Lake Michigan, but, as he discovered, a New York columnist dubbed Chicago the Windy City due to the citizenry's boasting about the 1893 World's Fair's firsts, including the introduction of the Ferris Wheel, Edison's moving picture camera, and a delightful new snack—Cracker Jack. *There is so much history connected to the World's Fair.* As the moon rose in the cloudy winter sky, the text started to blur.

Jake skimmed the pages, scanning for keywords, hoping something would pop out. Nothing specific came from any one book, but as he plowed through the tomes, a pattern did emerge: The Palmers' name was rarely mentioned without some reference to art or to the famed department store owner and philanthropist Marshall Field.

The Woman's Building, where Mary Cassatt's mural
was displayed during the World's Fair

Chapter 28

Sunday Evening (December 28th)

"*There* he is."

Jake woke with a start at the sound of Julie's voice. He lifted his head up from a dusty book and saw Julie, Ben, and Natalie entering the library.

"It's nearly curfew time, sleepyhead," Julie called.

"Must have dozed off. How long have I been up here?" Jake asked as he checked his watch: 9:30 P.M.

"Only about two hours, but when you didn't return by nine o'clock, we formed a search party," Ben said.

"Learn anything?" Natalie leaned over Jake's shoulder to look at the books.

"Maybe. Oh, I'm not sure."

"Walk us through it," Julie said.

"Well, members of the social and civic scene back then were really linked together. The Palmers were into real estate, dry goods, and art. Mrs. Palmer, Bertha, became an instrumental part of the Woman's Building at the World's Fair by organizing the exhibits and raising money. Somehow, Marshall Field fits into all of this, as well. He and Potter Palmer founded a store, and later Marshall took over the whole operation. It was called Marshall Field's, but it later became Macy's. Field was even friends with President Lincoln's son. These books are filled with stories and events about the prominence of these two families." Jake pushed the books into the middle of the table.

"What's with the notes?" Ben pointed to the yellow slips marking the pages.

"Just trying to piece things together," Jake replied.

Julie started opening the books to the marked pages. "Let's lay it all out for us to see."

The others huddled around the table and read the entries.

"This is interesting. It's a 1905 letter from William French, the director of the Art Institute, to Sara Hallowell, discussing where to put the murals from the fair," Natalie said.

"Who's Hallowell?" Ben asked.

"She was the art dealer that Bertha Palmer worked closely with," Jake replied.

"What else was happening around then?" Julie asked.

The kids started combing through the pages.

"Listen to this," Ben said. "In 1907, the Women's Tea Room on State Street opened its doors at Marshall Field's Department Store."

"This book says that 'Mr. Field had had high hopes that his store would serve as a cultural beacon. Unfortunately, he died the year before the tea room was complete,'" Natalie said.

"Okay, he may not have been there for the opening, but he would have been involved in the planning, right?" Julie offered. "So let's take an inventory. The Palmers and the Fields had been friends. They were businesspeople, heavily involved in real estate and Chicago's cultural life."

"Yes," Jake said. "And Bertha Palmer, the city's leading society matron, it says here, had access to all that artwork from the fair—pieces that she and her friend the art dealer were trying to locate homes for—"

Jake jumped up from his chair and ran around the side of the table. He snatched a book from Ben's hands and flipped back through to the section Ben had just read. "Women's Tea Room, 1907. Wouldn't it make sense to put a mural celebrating women in the *Women's* Tea Room?"

"Bertha lent the mural to Marshall Field!" they all said in unison.

"Yeah, but isn't that room now called the Walnut Room?" Natalie asked.

"It is. It's covered with wood paneling. My dad is always saying that often, what seems good on paper, turns out not to work when you have it constructed. So maybe they didn't like how the mural looked and covered the wall with walnut instead," Jake said, his teeth chattering with excitement.

"But why wouldn't they have returned the mural to Mrs. Palmer?" Ben asked.

"By that time, Bertha was out of the country. My book here says that she moved to London and didn't return until 1910. Maybe they tried to get a hold of her but couldn't," Julie suggested. "And perhaps the mural was so big that they couldn't locate another place as safe and secure as the wall in the tea room."

"What about documents or something else acknowledging the fact that the mural was there?" Ben asked.

"Maybe, but the store management was changing over to John Shedd at that time. It's conceivable the records were misplaced or lost during the shuffle. But why didn't my mom stumble on this? She was experienced at tracking down artwork," Jake said.

"Maybe she had, but then ruled Marshall Field's out as a wild goose chase," Ben said.

"Or perhaps she just approached it differently," Natalie said. "Your mom was basing her assumptions on firm facts, correspondence, and records. Our hypothesis is based on timing and happenstance: the mural needed a place to be

128

shown and the Marshall Field store was constructing a room that would benefit from the mural's presence," Natalie offered.

Dah-dah-dah da ta-da da ta-da. The kids' phones all chimed at the same time.

"The Dean is coming and it's past lights out," Julie whispered.

"Hide!" Jake grabbed a book and ran further into the library. The others followed, clearing the table of items in seconds and disappearing into the stacks of old books. Jake tried to slow his breathing and was worried the sound of his pounding heartbeat would alert the disciplinarian to his location. Lying prone on the floor behind a stack of ancient encyclopedias, Jake listened to the clack of the Dean's umbrella striking the floor. The sound grew louder with each step, echoing in Jake's ear. *He's right on top of me.*

The Dean's voice broke the eerie silence. "You, of all people, should know about the security cameras in this building, Mr. McGreevy. Discipline is not something you can pick or choose to have. You are either disciplined or you are not. It's ten minutes past curfew. You have three minutes to be in your rooms. Go."

As one, the kids emerged from their hiding spots. Without a word, or even chancing a glance at each other, they deposited the books onto the return shelf and hurried toward the door.

* * *

"So what I don't get is how Bronzer found me at the science museum?" Jake lifted his spoon out of the steaming hot oatmeal. "What do you think, Julie?"

Julie took a sip of juice. "That reporter talked about how we would be going to see the Art Institute and the Field Museum. So maybe he just staked it out."

"But why follow Jake at all?" Natalie asked.

"Probably worried he would find out about the mural. I mean, it's fake, right? Otherwise, why else?" Julie's voice squeaked as she asked the question.

"Julie's right. Why else? The painting *must* be a copy and my mom's hit-and-run was no *accident*." Jake dropped his spoon into his empty bowl. "We need to find the real mural."

"How are we going to do that, Jake?" Ben asked.

"Well, according to our itinerary, the school has organized a trip to various sites today and to Marshall Field's tonight after dinner, so we definitely won't have to sneak out." Jake smiled, happy about this lucky break. "Let me map out a quick plan. I'll share it with you guys over dinner."

Chapter 29

Monday Evening (December 29th)

The sun had set and the city's winter lights were already twinkling their festive welcome. The kids sat patiently on the idling bus, waiting to disembark. They had enjoyed a full day of sightseeing, with a break at Stanley House for dinner. Final stop: Marshall Field's.

Although it had been renamed Macy's in 2006, the theme of the store and its architecture had remained largely unchanged. Jake bounced back and forth between knowing, without a doubt, that the mural was in the Walnut Room and thinking he was ridiculous to even imagine such a thing.

The Walnut Room made sense. It was the only room in the store that hadn't gone through a major renovation in the past hundred years. Unfortunately, it was also the busiest place in the store. Dining in the Walnut Room, with its famed Christmas tree and elegant chandeliers, had become a tradition for Chicago natives and tourists alike.

"Did you see the weather forecast for tomorrow? We're supposed to be getting a huge ice storm," Natalie said as they sat on the bus. "Won't be until early tomorrow morning, but they predict it could be the storm of the century."

"That might be good for us. Hard to kick us out of camp if we're snowed in," Ben joked.

"Listen, I told you guys at dinner that I can easily do this alone," Jake whispered. "Instead of hiding out in the store when it closes, you can return on the bus with the rest of the school and I can search by myself."

Julie, who was sitting next to Jake, punched his leg.

"Ow!" Jake rubbed his knee.

"That's what you get for trying to ditch us. We're adults—well, sort of—and can make our own decisions. We could never desert you. And anyway, you need us!"

"She's right. Besides, you're always there for us. It's our turn to be there for you." Ben's genuine and thoughtful comment warmed Jake.

Once off the bus and free from supervision, if only for two hours, the kids from the camp moved together like sandpipers following a wave as they maneuvered into position to enter the store. Realizing that they could get separated in such a crowd, Jake looked up and pointed to the iconic bronze clock that jutted from the store's facade and hung over the sidewalk. "Look, if any one of us gets separated, return to this clock."

"Got it," the others responded. They followed the stream of shoppers seeking postholiday bargains into the massive department store.

"Okay, where to?" Julie asked as they absorbed the magnificent three-tiered fountain before them. Jake dug into his pocket and produced a quarter. "Need all the luck we can get," he said as he flipped the coin into the fountain. "If it's all right with you guys," Jake said, tucking his guidebook into his backpack, "I'd like to check out the Tiffany Favrile ceiling."

The others snickered and high-fived.

"What?"

"I made a bet that you were going to want to see that. But it was an easy bet. You're pretty predictable," Julie said, as she high-fived Ben again.

Wearing a shiny ski jacket, her wet hair glistening from the falling snow, Julie radiated sheer joy.

I'll give you predictable. Jake marched up to her, lifted up on his tiptoes, and kissed her squarely on the lips. It was a short kiss, but long enough to skyrocket his blood pressure.

"Did you see *that* coming?" Jake turned and strode off, attempting to appear relaxed, while every nerve in his body tingled.

*   *   *

As advertised, the Tiffany domed ceiling was spectacular. Most shoppers ignored the more than 1.6 million pieces of glass above their heads, but to Jake, the craftsmanship of the mosaic was mesmerizing and not to be missed.

"Don't strain your neck looking up, Jake," Ben commented.

"I'm short. My muscles are used to this," Jake shot back.

"It *is* beautiful," Julie said. "*È bellissimo.*" She stood next to Jake and he could feel her nervous energy. "What just happened back there?" she whispered.

Maybe I shouldn't have done that? Jake started quivering. *What if I just ruined my friendship with her? Should I tell her how I feel?* "Let's talk about it later—when we're alone," Jake muttered under his breath. He saw her nod and felt a wave of relief.

"If you're done gawking, Frank Lloyd, Natalie wants to do a bit of shopping," Ben called from across the crowded room.

Natalie gave Ben a playful tap. "Be nice."

Jake chuckled, knowing Ben actually meant it as a compliment, since he knew Jake liked being compared to his dad's favorite architect, Frank Lloyd Wright.

They followed Natalie as she wandered around the tables, choosing a pretty pin for her mom and a necktie with the Chicago skyline for her dad, who adored wearing conversational ties for the amusement of his dental patients. The others selected items as well and waited in line to pay. Too nervous to really get into shopping, Jake's only purchase was

133

an illustrated souvenir tin filled with Macy's famous Frango mint chocolates. Jake watched as Julie paid for some hand- and foot-warming packets.

"My feet were freezing on the bus ride over here," she mumbled as the clerk handed her the packages.

"OK, let's go have some dessert in the Walnut Room to scope it out." Jake absently reached for Julie's hand and found comfort in the warmth of her fingers. Although Christmas had passed, the Walnut Room remained open and busy. White linen tablecloths, a vibrant red carpet, dark walnut walls, and a forty-foot sparkling Christmas tree created the perfect ambiance for a special meal.

"Wow, no wonder this place has been popular for a century," Julie said.

After waiting in line for nearly an hour, the kids sat down at a table near the Christmas tree.

"Looks like this tree is sitting on some sort of platform." Ben leaned over and lifted the cloth skirt that was draped over the platform. "It's just a bunch of tables pushed together. I bet we can hide under there until the store closes."

The kids paid for their desserts and one by one bent over as if they were tying their shoe laces; then they disappeared underneath the tree's skirt. Jake was the last to go and had to wait for several minutes until all of the waiters and other patrons were looking elsewhere. As he ducked under, a young boy saw him and pointed. Jake winked at the tot and placed a single finger in front of his lips. The boy grinned and Jake's heart started beating again,

Now all we have to do is wait. As Jake tried to be patient, he flipped on the flashlight and investigated the odds and ends around them. "Look at this," he whispered as he grabbed a twenty-four-ounce bottle.

"What?" Julie replied.

"Fog juice. It's a mix of vegetable glycerin and water used in fog machines. They must use it for one of the Christmas displays," Jake said as he stuffed the bottle into the mesh side-pocket of his backpack.

"Cool." Ben turned to check it out.

"Boys," Julie and Natalie grumbled.

*   *   *

Another hour—or an eternity if you're crammed into a small area wearing bulky winter clothing—passed without incident.

"Sounds like the staff is done cleaning up the restaurant. Let's go," Jake finally whispered. The others crawled out and stretched their legs.

"Search quickly! I'm sure the Dean realizes we're missing by now," Jake said.

"I wouldn't be surprised if the U.S. Marshalls are being called in to find us," Ben joked.

"I know. I feel bad about the Dean, though. I think he took the Matthews kid's disappearance really hard," Jake said.

Spreading out around the massive room, the kids each went to their preassigned wall. Jake reached his section and brushed his hand against the rich dark wood. *No indication of a way to remove the panel.* Jake's heart pounded. *I had hoped there would be some hinges or screws or something. The mural has to be here, but how will we find out without damaging the walnut?*

"Nothing is standing out," Julie called and strode over to Jake. The others followed her, and the kids all sat at a table in the corner of the room.

"I kept feeling around the edges of the panels, but they are firmly mounted to the wall and I can't see any way of removing them," Jake lamented.

"I noticed along the bottom there was a very small gap between the wood and the wall," Julie said.

"I saw that, too. I tried to stick my camera phone up there, but there's not enough space, Natalie said.

Jake attached his fiber-optic camera to his phone and pulled out his flashlight.

"I see where you're going. Will this help?" Natalie reached into her shoulder bag and produced a dental mirror.

"I'm impressed. You just happen to have a dental mirror in your purse?"

"My dad has a ton of them and gave me one since I keep dropping stuff between car seats and such. It's handy for that and all sorts of other things."

"Well, it's *perfect*," Jake said as he handed his Maglite to Natalie. She bounced the beam off the mirror, angling it so a ray of light shone perfectly between the wall and the wood paneling.

Traversing the entire room, with stops every few minutes to listen if anyone was coming, the four of them searched each wall.

"Last one," Julie muttered.

Jake bit his bottom lip. All they'd found so far was gum shoved behind the panels and a hundred spiders. *It has to be here.*

Suddenly, the image of chalk-white walls and dark panels changed. Displayed on the camera's screen was what appeared to be a curled edge of paper.

Chapter 30

Monday Evening (December 29th)

"What's that?" the gang gasped in unison.

"Could it be the corner of the mural?" Jake's voice squeaked.

"Let's see how far it goes." Julie fired up the step-counter app on her phone. The four of them moved slowly along the wall. The curled paper edge continued with each step and Jake's pulse increased pace by pace. As quickly as it had appeared, the image changed back to nothing.

"Looks like fifty-eight feet, give or take," Julie said.

"Crud. The mural is sixty-four feet wide." Jake's throat tightened.

The others looked as dejected as he felt. *We've done so much for nothing.*

"Wait a minute. I thought I read about the painting having a border," Ben said as he dug into his bag for his computer. His fingers flurried as he tapped into the knowledge of the world.

"The painting was adorned with a three-foot border on each side," Ben read.

"Sixty-four feet minus three feet on both sides is fifty-eight!" The dangerous emotion of hope flooded Jake's heart. "We need a sample," Jake said as he dropped his backpack.

"You're going to *cut* a hundred-year-old Mary Cassatt painting?" Natalie asked.

"Not an ideal move, I know, but how else will we convince someone to investigate? Everyone thinks the real mural is in the museum, so without some actual proof, we'll have nothing," Jake responded. "Besides, professional restorers can easily patch something like this." *I hope so, at least.*

Pulling out his Leatherman, Jake walked over to a table and picked up two dinner knives. Grabbing his duct tape, *the second-best invention after the Leatherman*, he affixed a knife to each jaw of the Leatherman's built-in pliers.

"I get it. You've just made a really long set of needle-nose pliers," Ben said.

Jake nodded and headed back to the wall. Going more by feel than what he could see, he slid the pliers behind the panel.

"If you misjudged the gap there, your pliers will be stuck with the mural for another hundred years," Ben said.

"Thanks, pal. That really takes the pressure off," Jake replied.

After a few grunts, Jake removed the pliers from the wall. Snagged in its teeth was a five-inch strip of canvas.

"Careful. I bet it's brittle," Julie said.

Despite being faded and covered in dirt, thick paint lines were clearly visible on the canvas.

"I think we found it," Jake said in a calm, even tone.

"You don't seem excited," Natalie said.

"My mother spent her life looking for this. She died because of it. I don't know if I like the mural or hate it."

Julie wrapped her arm around Jake. "It's beautiful, because finding it will mean that whoever killed your mom will be brought to justice. She would be happy at this moment, and so should you."

Jake nodded. He pulled out his empty thermos, shook any lingering water droplets out, stuffed it with some Kleenex so the piece wouldn't get lodged at the bottom, and then gently placed the canvas inside. "That should protect it long enough to get it to the right people."

SLAM!

The sound of the doors banging open behind them startled the group. Swiveling, Jake saw Bronzer—accompanied by five other goons—blocking the exit.

Ben stepped in front of Natalie to shield her. Simultaneously, Jake stepped behind Julie.

"How chivalrous," Julie muttered.

"I have a plan," Jake whispered. "Buy some time, Ben." Jake wrenched the fog juice from his backpack.

"Our school group is waiting for us," Ben called to the men.

"Nice try. We saw your friends leave an hour ago," Bronzer sneered.

In a matter of seconds, Jake popped off the bottle's cap, yanked the hand warmers from Julie's purse, crushed the packages to activate the product, and shoved them into the fog juice. He then screwed the cap back on and jabbed a hole in it with the knife blade from his Leatherman.

"Grenade!" he called as he tossed the bottle at the men. Before the bottle had even left his hand, smoke from the reaction of heat and glycerin started spewing from the lid. Landing on the floor by the thugs, the bottle spun around, rapidly disgorging plumes of thick fog.

"Run!" Julie grabbed Jake's hand and pushed on Ben and Natalie. The kids leapfrogged over the tables surrounding the Christmas tree and sprinted past the men.

"Split up!" Jake called. He could already hear the men's footsteps rumbling from the room. He and Julie ran into the housewares section on the seventh floor.

"Where are the stairs?" Julie cried.

"There!" Jake pointed to a sign.

They ran toward the door, but a goon appeared in the aisle, blocking the exit.

Jake ducked out of the man's reach and crashed into a table displaying kitchenware, sending pots, pans, and hand-held appliances flying. The sound of metal hitting the floor echoed through the store. The man pulled a knife and Jake grabbed the closest weapon, a cordless hand mixer. The man jabbed at him, but Jake parried the blow with the mixer. The man lunged again. This time, the blade was caught in the spinning beaters. Two hundred and twenty watts of force twisted the knife from the man's hand. Then Julie smacked him on the back of the head with a frying pan and he stumbled to the ground.

"Nice!" Jake grabbed her and ran for the exit. Tearing through the door, they rounded stairway after stairway until they burst into the cosmetics area on the first floor. A flash of movement caught Jake's eye, and he felt a sudden stinging pain in the head. Then, darkness.

Chapter 31

Monday Evening (December 29th)

"I think he's coming around," a faint voice said.

In a foggy haze, Jake felt a cold chill as his brain pounded its way to consciousness. He realized he was lying on a cold surface with his hands tied behind his back at the wrists. It was pitch black except for a slit of light coming in from a baseball-sized hole above them. The ground felt metallic.

"Is everyone okay?"

"Other than being tied up, yes," Julie said.

In the dimly lit space, Jake realized the others were all similarly bound.

"Two guys nabbed Natalie and me as we were heading toward the exit. I saw some security guards lying on the ground near the doors. The thugs must have taken them out," Ben said.

"And when you and I came through the door on the main floor, Bronzer hit you on the head and one of his cronies grabbed me. I tried to fight but they were too strong and there were just too many of them." Julie's voice told Jake more about their dire situation than what he could discern from his surroundings.

"Are we in some sort of shipping container?" Jake asked.

"Yes. They loaded us into this big metal box," Natalie explained.

"Where's Bronzer?" Jake asked.

"We heard them say something about getting a truck back here to get the container," Julie said.

"We've got to get out of here before they return." Jake's heart started thumping.

"I know, but these ropes are too strong. We need a knife or something sharp," Ben said.

"My new belt! There's a compartment with a knife in it." Jake rolled onto his back and slid his hands down toward his feet. "My arms are disproportionally long compared to my legs." Jake grunted and managed to get his bound hands past his feet. With his hands now in front of him, he quickly pulled on the belt buckle, triggering the secret compartment. He grabbed the knife and carefully opened the blade. "Julie, you're closest. Shimmy over here."

Julie flopped around until her restraints were within Jake's reach. *Don't cut her.* Moments later, she was freed. She took the knife and cut the ropes binding the others.

Jake stood up and stretched, and as blood returned to the area on his head where he'd been struck, he felt a throbbing pain. "I assume they took everything?" Jake felt his pockets for any gear.

"Yes. Phones, backpacks, my computer—all of it," Ben said.

"OK. Lift me up," Jake said.

Ben hoisted Jake onto his shoulders. Jake pressed his face against the container door and tried to look out through the hole. As his head brushed the wall, it grazed the bruise from Bronzer's blow. Pain pushed a slight whimper through his lips.

"We're in some sort of warehouse. Seems empty and I don't see anyone around." Pushing harder against the door until bits of rust dug into his skin, he peered down at the locking mechanism. "Good. They're lazy crooks."

"What do you mean?" Julie asked.

"The center locking bar—the post that you lift, turn, and then drop back down to lock the doors—is still partially turned. If we can pull it up, the door might open." Jake dropped from Ben's shoulders.

"Tell us what to do." Julie stood up.

"I need everyone's shoe laces." Jake bent to unlace his own shoes. After collecting each set of laces, he tied them in a long chain using a double fisherman's knot. He removed his belt— Ben provided his, as well—and formed a loop, securing it to the laces with a bowline knot. "The belts are stiffer than the laces, so they'll be easier to loop over the bar." Jake stood and walked to the door. He climbed back up onto Ben's shoulders and prepared to cram the poor-man's lasso through the hole.

Jake pushed the cord through the gap. It was difficult to see and manage the rope at the same time, so he tried to go more by feel. The belt bumped up against the door as it swung back and forth.

"Sounds like it's not low enough. Let out some more slack," Ben said.

"I don't have anymore. Lower me down."

Jake climbed off Ben's shoulders to take an inventory of his gear. *Boots—already took the laces. Belts—already in use. Jacket—wouldn't fit through the hole. Mittens.* "Mittens!" Jake pulled the new pair from his coat pocket. *Glad the weavers double-layered them.* "These'll work!"

Jake unraveled the mittens, and the yarn spooled onto the floor. When he affixed the yarn to the shoelaces, the gang reassembled into their assigned positions.

After a few more swings, he felt a slight tug. "I think I have it."

"Slowly then," Julie called.

My thought exactly. Hand-over-hand, Jake cautiously brought the laces back through the hole. When it felt tight, he applied steady even pressure.

"I think I hear it moving!" Ben said.

"Shh. I want to hear it release, so we know when the door will move. I don't want to tumble out," Jake said. The grinding noise of the metal locking bar sliding up from its home echoed inside the container.

CLUNK. The door swung open.

Spanning the size of a football field, the space held nothing other than the shipping container and some empty cardboard boxes.

"Rats. No sign of our stuff," Jake said as he scanned the area.

"Looks like those are the only doors." Julie pointed to a large sliding door that would allow trucks to enter, and a pedestrian door off to its right. The kids ran over and found both securely locked.

"What about that window?" Ben motioned to a broken window approximately twenty feet above the ground. He trotted over to the wall. It was aluminum siding held in place by wooden two-by-fours that ran horizontally every two feet. "Perfect. It's a pole barn. Might as well be a climbing wall. We can scale it easily enough and escape out the window."

As effortlessly as if it were a ladder, Ben scurried up the side of the building. "Yep, there's a snow bank formed by a plow from a previous storm. We can jump into it," he called.

"What's wrong, Natalie?" Jake asked when he saw the nervous look on her face.

"My fear of heights. I can't do it. Being up that high will make me so dizzy, I'll let go or something. Plus you guys are strong from rock climbing and Julie is a super gymnast. These spindly arms"—Natalie held them out to demonstrate—"are great for violin, but I don't think I can climb up there."

Ben returned to the warehouse floor. "I can carry you."

"Maybe you guys can just escape and come back with help?" Natalie suggested.

"No way we're leaving you. Ben's right. He can carry you. I saw him carry a huge backpack up a steep trail we hiked during fall break in the Adirondacks."

Jake tied their linked belts around Natalie and looped the strap over Ben, forming a makeshift harness. "This won't hold all of your weight, so you'll still need to hold Ben tight."

"Given my problem with heights, I'll have no problem at all with that!" Natalie said.

"Here we go," Ben said as he mounted the wall with Natalie on his back. Hand over hand, he slowly climbed. He grunted a few times but was able to make steady progress up the side of the building.

"Wish I could do that," Jake muttered to Julie.

"Don't stress. We all have different strengths. Your brain is mightier than other people's brawn," Julie replied.

"Thanks." *But I think I'll still add more weight training to my workout routine.*

Ben and Natalie reached the window. Using her elbow, Natalie knocked out the glass pane and Ben helped her climb through it. After a bit of prodding, Natalie dropped into the snow bank on the other side.

"She's good!" Ben gave a thumbs-up and disappeared through the window.

Climbing next to each other, Jake and Julie quickly ascended the wall. Julie went first through the window. Jake leapt from the building and landed in the snow. Rolling down the plow-made hill, he took in a mouthful of snow.

"Yuck!" He spat the icy flakes from his mouth as he stood up and dusted himself off.

They were welcomed into the winter night by a mix of freezing rain and heavy snow.

"Looks like the storm came early," Natalie said.

Explains why Bronzer isn't back yet—bad roads. Jake and the others trudged down the sidewalk. The light from the lamp-posts shone onto the white snow, creating an eerie glow along the desolate block. There were no cars on the road and all of the buildings were dark. *No help out here. This is like a bad movie.* Thoroughly soaked, the gang hiked six blocks before finding the first street sign.

"This is 47th and Lawrence. Hannah's place is on Lawrence. Come on. I say we go this way." Jake stuffed his freezing hands into his wet coat pockets.

Chapter 32

Monday Evening (December 29th)

The group walked in silence for twenty minutes until Ben spoke. "It's official. This is the coldest and most miserable I have *ever* been."

"Just focus on Hannah's hot cocoa," Jake muttered.

"Oh, yeah. Hope she still has marshmallows." Ben picked up the pace.

"Boys," the girls sighed.

"Hey, there it is!" Jake called. He tried to run, but his feet were suddenly level with his chest. "Careful—it's slick," he moaned from the ground.

Gingerly, the others helped him up, and they skated more than walked up the pathway to the retirement home.

After being buzzed in, the kids tried to stomp the snow from their feet.

"Oh, my goodness!" Hannah exclaimed when she saw the bedraggled group. Jake gave a rapid recap of the situation as Hannah alternated between hugging the kids and placing her hand over her heart.

"And what happened to your mittens, Jake? Your hands are nearly frostbitten," Hannah said.

"We had to unravel them to . . . oh, no!" Fear coursed through Jake's veins. "I left the mittens and the tag with the retirement home's name on it in the container. Bronzer will know where to find us!"

"We'll call the police right now." Hannah marched to the nearby phone. Jake couldn't hear what the police were saying, but whatever it was, it wasn't good, and Hannah's face soured with each exchange.

"At first, they thought it was another false alarm, like Mr. Perlmutter's the other day," she explained after hanging up, "but I think I may have convinced them. Anyway, they agreed to send a squad car as soon as they can spare one. They say they have hundreds of accidents to attend to."

"In other words, it could be a while," Jake said.

"Right. So can't we just barricade the doors?" Natalie asked.

"These guys don't strike me as the type to give up easily. Anyway, even if we block the doors, there are lots of windows large enough for them to break and climb through. We could never stop them." Jake's mind started calculating.

He jogged over to a floor map of the facility posted on the wall. Laid out as a pentagon, the building had five public areas. The lobby, on one side of the pentagon, welcomed visitors with some comfortable chairs, a coffee and a hot cocoa station, and bulletin boards filled with announcements and pictures of active seniors. If you turned left off the lobby, you passed by the administrative offices and arrived at the kitchen and dining area. The next side of the pentagon held an arts and crafts center. The fitness center was next, and the last side of the facility before completing the loop back to the lobby was the dayroom where the kids had played their music.

Jake took a sip of the steaming hot cocoa and closed his eyes for a moment. It scalded his tongue, but he tuned out the pain as he focused on the battle plan unfolding in his head. Jake turned to the group. "Assemble some volunteers and tell everyone else to lock themselves in their rooms."

*   *   *

Jake stood on a chair and surveyed the crowd. Representatives from each group—the veterans, weavers, kitchen staff, and others—waited for Jake to detail the plan. *They're all looking to me to tell them what to do.* Jake glanced over at Julie, who gave him an encouraging smile. *I can't fail them.* He felt his courage rise, and he squared his shoulders. He and the other kids had debated the plan for a few minutes before agreeing on a solution—a solution that he hoped would lead to victory.

"Thank you all for volunteering. I know this isn't your fight and you didn't invite danger into your home, so we are personally very grateful that you came."

A few of the residents nodded.

"Here's what I'm thinking. We need to funnel the bad guys through the different common areas starting with the cafeteria, then the arts and crafts room, followed by the fitness center, and finally the dayroom. Each spot will have its own surprises, and if we're lucky, we'll slow them down until the police arrive."

Murmurs cascaded through the crowd.

"Won't they have guns?" one of the weavers called.

Jake gulped. "Most likely, but we are hoping to disarm them. My friend Natalie has a thought on that."

Natalie hopped up onto a chair. "I was thinking we'd build a large magnet and suck their weapons away, perhaps into a front-loading washing machine where the door locks until the cycle is complete."

A resident holding a white cane with a red tip waved. "I was an electrician. If you'll be my eyes, I can help you, sweetheart."

"Great!" Natalie escorted the man away.

"Ben, take the staff and whip up a sticky treat in the kitchen," Jake instructed.

"Yes, sir. Ciabatta charm coming right up." Ben swiveled and led the staff toward the kitchen.

"Julie, you're with the weavers. Please knit up a welcome."

"Got it!" Julie led about a dozen women armed with giant knitting bags.

"Hannah, you'll be in the fitness center. Prepare to pump some iron toward our guests."

Hannah motioned for a few men to follow her.

Jake turned to the remaining men, the veterans. Each man wore his unit's cap decked out with different pins. Some men actually wore their service uniform. The faded khaki and olive drab, better known as OD green, conveyed a strength that would have otherwise been lacking in this emergency situation.

"Gentlemen—" Jake heard someone clear his throat. He then noticed two women dressed in Women's Army Corp uniforms. Thinking back to his history class, Jake realized these ladies were two of the first women, other than nurses, to serve in the army.

"My apologies. I am truly honored to be here with you, and I appreciate your service. This fight will pale in comparison with those you've seen, but it will still be dangerous. You'll be the last line of defense. If we fail—well, it won't be good."

Jake reached for his Leatherman but paused when he realized it wasn't attached to his belt. *I need my backpack.* "We found some tools in the maintenance closet but we still need more. Do any of you have pliers, knives, or anything of use?"

A few people raised their hands. One gentleman, an African American wearing a Vietnam veteran's hat, caught Jake's attention. Jake's pulse raced as he ran over to the man. "Sir, is that what I think it is?"

"Sergeant Major Johnson, U.S. Army, retired, Jake. And yes, it is," the man said in a playful tone.

"May I see that?" Jake held out his hand.

The man placed a Leatherman in his palm. "I received this in 1983 when I retired after thirty years of service."

"It's the PST, Pocket Survival Tool, the first ever Leatherman."

"You know your tools, son."

"Yes, sir."

"Take it. From what Hannah's told me, it sounds like you'll do more good with it than I."

Jake nodded. "Would you help me organize the troops?"

"My pleasure." The man puffed up. Despite his age, his voice boomed throughout the lobby. "Platoon, ten-hut!"

All of the veterans, even those in wheelchairs, stiffened their posture and prepared for his next command.

"Left-face!"

The group turned to its left.

"For-ward!"

"Forward," the veterans echoed.

"March!"

At more of a shuffle than a march, the men and women moved toward the dayroom.

Chapter 33

Monday Evening (December 29th)

On a previous visit, Jake had toured the dining area and remembered being impressed with its décor: rich carpet, vibrant wall colors, and floor-length curtains gave it a warm feeling. Holiday decorations still adorned the tables and the buffet. But now the room had been transformed, and it resembled a fortress more than a splendid eating area. Overturned tables formed giant walls; only a thin gap allowed passage from the entrance hallway and corridor that led to the arts and crafts room.

"Wow," Jake called to Ben as he entered the room.

"Yeah, I think so, too. They generally seem excited to help and are actually enjoying themselves." Ben waved his arm at the crowd of seniors busily pushing furniture around.

"I like it. That's a good choke point. I assume I'll lead the thugs through it?" Jake said.

"Yes, and then bam, the pots and pans will swing down from the ceiling and clobber them." Ben pointed above them where several staff members had removed the false ceiling panels, exposing the plumbing and electrical conduits. They were busy tying ropes, fashioned from extension cords, from water pipes to kitchenware handles.

"Good. But won't they just dodge them?" Jake asked as he walked between the piles of furniture.

"No, the place where we're standing will be covered with my super-sticky dough. They'll be stuck for only a moment, but that should be all we need to give them a cast-iron welcome."

"But how will *I* make it over the dough?"

"On this sled." Ben held up a large cookie sheet smothered in vegetable oil. "You'll glide right over the ciabatta."

"Anything else?"

"Soda fountain—extreme edition." Ben escorted Jake over to the self-serve carbonated beverage station. The cabinet doors were open, revealing the silver CO_2 canisters. "We can hook some thin hoses directly to the bottles and bypass the regulation valve."

"What PSI are you forecasting?" Jake asked.

"Normally these tanks run one hundred pounds per square inch, but with the thinner tubing and no valve control, I think we can double it."

"Good thing you aced Mr. Hickman's physics class," Jake laughed.

"I don't know if that's it, or hanging out with you too much."

"Either way, Natalie will be impressed." Jake gave Ben a punch on the arm before hustling to the arts and crafts room.

The once peaceful room was now a spider's web of knitting. Spread across the floor was a large net made of yarn. Women, with needles flashing, surrounded the net, adding foot after foot and layer after layer.

"Great work."

"We're triple layering it to contain whomever we snare." Julie stood off to the side.

"How about the paint bombs I suggested?" Jake asked.

"Complete." Julie pointed to a stack of clay pots neatly lined up behind some overturned tables. "We filled the small pots with paint and then taped some paper over the tops to hold the paint inside during flight. The person on the receiving end will get a sting from the jar and be covered instantly," Julie said.

"Couldn't have done it better myself." Jake gave her a quick grin.

The fitness center was spacious and modern. One side of the wall was lined with mirrors and various weight machines. The other side of the room contained elliptical trainers, exercise bikes, and other cardio equipment. Several flat-screen televisions streamed news coverage of the massive storm pounding Chicago. Jake scanned each machine. Weights, pulleys, electric motors—it was like a giant erector set. *Jackpot.* Jake rubbed his hands together—still cold from their walk— as he plotted next steps in his mind.

"Jake," Hannah called. "This is Tom. He was a mechanic for Chicago Public Works. He's got lots of experience with machinery."

"Glad to have you helping out." Jake pumped Tom's hand. After a quick exchange of ideas, they lifted the rear portions of the treadmills and faced them toward the hallway coming from the craft room.

"What's the max speed?" Jake asked.

"Twelve miles per hour," Tom responded.

Jake ball-parked the math in his head. "So about 17 feet per second. Should be enough to pack a wallop."

"I'll go find a bunch of small hard items to drop onto the belt." Hannah turned to walk away.

"Get some bed sheets, too. We'll use them to hold the ammo above the treadmills until the right time," Jake called after her before returning to the task at hand. "The bicep-triceps pulley systems—" Jake directed Tom to a freestanding weight machine that had a pulley attached to a set of weight plates, where the user would stand and pull down on a handle and lift the weights. "We could rig another surprise for anyone not caught in the initial volley."

"I see where you're going with this," Tom said, nodding.

"And what about the elliptical trainers?" Jake asked. "If we take out a few bolts on the arm levers, we could essentially create a machine that will punch anyone nearby," he said.

"Right. The person will dodge to the right and end up by this machine." Tom simulated jumping out of the path of the treadmills. "Then the elliptical starts up and the arms will smack 'em. We'll get on it." Tom motioned to a few other seniors who had volunteered to help.

"Great. I'm going to check on the veterans." Jake sprinted down the hallway toward the dayroom, where he immediately got to work on key parts of their plan. Using only the Leatherman and a few tools, Jake and several of the men created air guns by combining walkers and canes with oxygen bottles. Taping the tennis balls, already affixed to the walkers, Jake ensured a good seal. *The air pressure will launch these balls with high velocity.* He surveyed the other preparations. Alka-Seltzer tablets were piled next to twenty-ounce water bottles, and motorized wheelchairs—with crutches mounted as battering rams—sat in the corner and awaited the modern-day joust. *Looking good here.*

"Amazing what motivated people can do in a short time," Jake exclaimed. A man in a wheelchair lifted his hand to catch Jake's attention. *He can barely move, yet he's out here to help.* The man—Jake thought he looked like a Native American— wore a Marine Corps World War II uniform, and his hat read 6th Marine Division.

"Yes, sir." Jake leaned in so he could hear the man better.

"We could have used your type of ingenuity on Sugar Loaf Hill. We were down to throwing rocks at the enemy." The man lightly patted Jake's hands.

Jake didn't even try to hold back the tears that welled up in his eyes. "I . . . thank you. I am honored by that. And thank you for coming out to help."

"One more thing. It's okay to be afraid. Courage is not the absence of fear. It's acting in spite of it," the man said.

Overcome by fatigue and emotion, Jake nodded, and tried to slow his breathing. These people were banding together for him, a stranger. Jake vowed to volunteer in the retirement home near his house, assuming he made it out of this mess in one piece. Satisfied that everything was progressing, Jake turned and jogged back through each room in the circuit, ending back in the lobby. He found Natalie on her knees with her arms inside a front-loading washing machine.

"How's it going?" Jake asked.

"I think Natalie here is a natural," the blind man said from a nearby chair.

"She took a five-pound dumbbell and wrapped it in about a mile of wire that we found in the maintenance closet. She then rigged it to the power of this washing machine that we dragged to the lobby."

"All done." Natalie pulled her head out of the machine. "And it wasn't that easy. Harold here knows his stuff. Even though he retired before these kinds of washers came out, he knew how to guide me through the circuitry and such."

"Have you tested it?" Jake peered inside to see the ball of copper wire and dumbbell.

"I was just about to." Natalie plugged the machine into the wall.

Jake felt a strong tug on his belt and the Leatherman PST flew from his waist directly into the washing machine, slamming it against the inside with a loud bang. *Oh, no! The sergeant major's retirement gift!*

Natalie turned the power off and Jake reached his hand into the machine.

"Good. It's not scratched," Jake said.

"We'll mount a pulley on the door, so you can close it once the guns are inside. When the washing cycle starts, the door will remain sealed shut, even though there won't be any water. We added a battery to the locking mechanism, so even if they cut the power, it will still take twenty minutes for the door to unlock. We couldn't make it any longer because the battery won't last that long. We thought about staying here in the lobby so we could retrieve the guns, but there are no lockable closets or any other secure areas to hide away in," Natalie said.

"So worst case, they won't have access to their guns for twenty minutes?"

"That's right. But it will be a fast twenty minutes if they're chasing you through the building," Natalie responded.

"Let's hope it's enough."

Chapter 34

Tuesday (Just Past Midnight, December 30th)

Despite three more calls to the police, nobody had hope at this point that they'd arrive before the goons. Jake sat alone in the lobby trying to focus on the plan, but he couldn't stop thinking about his mother. *What would she think about all of this?* Jake smiled. *Considering her cleverness in stashing the notebook behind the sconce, I bet she'd be helping us right now.* Jake heard someone prying the door open. He stood and bit his bottom lip, hoping to see the telltale blue of a police uniform. Instead, he saw Bronzer and five burly men.

The men stopped just inside and stared at Jake. Despite being twenty feet away, the pistols in their hands loomed large. *Can't run. Need them to get a little closer to the washing machine.* Thankfully, none of the men looked to their right where the hungry mouth of the front-loading washer was waiting.

I need them all to hold their weapons out so the magnet will work better. He spotted his backpack in Bronzer's hand. "That's my backpack," Jake seethed.

"Had to bring it, so we can bury it with you." Bronzer tossed the pack to the side.

"You killed my mother. For what, some forged painting?" Jake glared at him.

Bronzer raised his gun and the others followed suit. "She was too nosy. You're just like her," he growled.

Courage is not the absence of fear; it's acting in spite of it. Here we go. Jake grinned. "I'm beginning to learn that." He plugged the extension cord ends together, triggering the magnet. Although not as powerful as Luke Skywalker's force, the magnetic pull was a close second, and it ripped the guns from the unsuspecting thugs' hands.

"Hey, what—?" they shouted.

CLANG!

The metal pistols lodged inside the washing machine. Jake jerked the cord, and the door slammed shut. He ran toward the dining room.

At a full sprint, Jake jumped onto the cookie sheet. *Whoa! This is faster than I thought it would be.* He tried to maintain his balance as the sled shot across the field of dough. Jake tumbled off the pan on the other side of the ciabatta.

"We've got you now!" Bronzer yelled as he stepped onto the white sticky surface. Immediately, he and the others tripped, their feet coming out of their shoes as the dough held firm. They struggled to their feet and their efforts were rewarded with a cavalcade of pots and pans swinging from the ceiling.

BONG!

Hitting them in the head and shoulders, the pans swung back and forth, levying blow after blow. Falling back to the ground, they were again ensnared by the dough.

"Now!" Jake waved his arms.

Ben and Natalie popped up from behind a table holding the soda hoses. A loud hissing sound preceded a shower of cola.

"Argh!" the men cried as they were doused in sticky syrup.

"Archers!" Jake yelled.

Having removed the sneeze guards from the buffet line, Jake and the others rigged suspenders as makeshift slingshots.

Several residents stood up and launched dishes at the gang members. They hit one of them on the side of the head with a serving platter, and he withered under the blow. Another had a marble-filled teapot slam his knee and buckled under the pain.

"Yee-haw. Look at 'em fall!" one of the residents called out.

Despite the onslaught of tableware, the men continued toward Jake.

"Time to boogie." Jake nodded toward the door. He, Ben, and Natalie ducked under the stream of dishes and sprinted for the exit.

Some of the men headed toward the seniors manning the buffet table.

"Leave them—get the kids!" Bronzer called.

*   *   *

Jake squinted as he entered the arts and crafts room. Bright lights, normally used for projects requiring detailed work, were focused on the entrance.

"Over here," Julie called.

His eyes still recovering, Jake allowed Julie to pull him and the others into position.

"How'd it go?" Julie whispered.

"Everything worked but they didn't flee. We're not inflicting enough pain to deter them," Jake responded.

Footsteps thundered from the hallway. The men stopped abruptly, blinded by the lights.

"Now!" Julie screamed, causing Jake to jump.

A huge colorful net, weighted down by dumbbells borrowed from the fitness room, dropped from the ceiling and covered all six men.

They fought to free themselves, yelling at each other and at the kids. Julie whistled and several seniors rose up from behind the tables and threw clay pots of paint at the trapped men. Jake and the others joined in the bombardment. Throwing as hard as he could, Jake hurled pot after pot at their assailants, who were cursing under the net. Soon the men and the room were a collage of colors.

"Looks like they're getting loose!" Natalie yelled.

"Persistent bunch," Jake muttered. *We're nearly out of pots.* Jake signaled the residents to retreat to the relative safety of their rooms.

"Come on. Let's hope the fitness room works out." Jake's attempt at a joke didn't lighten the gravity of the situation.

*　　*　　*

Hannah and Tom were waiting at the far end of the room behind the treadmills.

"They're right behind us!" Jake called as he joined them.

"We're ready." Hannah's face was the picture of pure determination.

Moments later, the brutes burst into the room. With a shriek, Hannah pulled on the string, and the sheets released their cargo. Miscellaneous objects shot from the treadmills like cannon balls. Many bounced harmlessly off the weight equipment, while others careened into the mirrored walls, shattering them. Yet the cries of pain signaled that some items had hit their marks. One man caught a weighted running shoe in the forehead and fell over backwards. Another attacker took a CD alarm clock to the gut, the air whooshing from his lungs as he doubled over. Two men, attempting to jump away from the flying junk, got caught in a tripwire. Recognition followed by fear crossed their faces. Then three hundred pounds of weights dropped from the bicep machine as the wire on the floor snapped tight. The wire caught the men in the groin, and they squealed in high-pitched tones as it lifted them into the air. Another group ducked behind the elliptical trainer. Then Tom plugged the extension cord into the nearby wall socket, sending power to the modified machines. The arms of the exercise equipment came to life and the men, momentarily confused by the chaos, took a savage beating.

When the last of the projectiles had shot from the treadmill, the room became still. The only sound was the soft groans of the gang members, all lying on the floor.

We did it!

That momentary spark of hope vanished from Jake's mind as the men slowly picked themselves up from the floor. Bronzer, despite a nasty head wound, looked as fierce as ever.

"Fall back," Jake whispered, his throat suddenly dry.

Hannah and Tom locked themselves in a maintenance closet as the kids, better suited for running, tore through the hallway away from the danger.

Chapter 35

Tuesday (One Hour Past Midnight, December 30th)

Jake tried to slow his breath as he hid behind one of the overturned tables in the dayroom. The lights had been turned off and only a sliver of red from the exit sign saved the room from complete darkness. Jake felt the reassuring grip of the sergeant major's hand on his shoulder.

The goons crept into the room.

"Find the lights—but be careful," Bronzer snarled.

The fluorescent ceiling lights flickered and hummed as they warmed up. The six men, covered in paint, blood, and bruises, stood in the middle of the room, bewildered at the sight surrounding them. A warm feeling shot through Jake's veins as he too gazed upon the scene: thirty men and two women, wearing their respective military branches' baseball caps, stood grim-faced and stoic.

"Oh, no," one of the thugs sighed.

"Platoon, open fire!" the sergeant major barked.

As one, the first rank of veterans lifted their stainless steel canes and walkers. The hiss of the oxygen filling the metal tubes replaced the silence. Staccato popping sounds filled the room as the air pressure dislodged the tennis balls. Dozens of the projectiles screamed across the room, the cries of the attackers letting the soldiers know when their aim was true. The six men tried to duck and weave as the projectiles shot past them.

"Grenades!" Jake shouted.

The second group of veterans dropped dozens of Alka-Seltzer tablets into the twenty-ounce water bottles, spun the caps on, and then launched them at the men.

BOOM!

The water explosions disoriented the men and they stumbled to the ground.

"Tanks!" the sergeant major yelled.

Unmanned motorized wheelchairs with crutches mounted as battering rams sped toward the men. One crutch caught a goon square in the chest, the satisfying crack of his ribs echoing above the chaos. Another chair swept a man's legs, sending him to the ground. The last homemade tank slammed into the back of a thug and he toppled over.

"Mines!" Jake called.

A group of men used shuffleboard cues to slide their bedpan pucks across the floor, tripping several men.

"Charge!" Jake picked up a cane and ran toward the criminals. The veterans followed, and the crowd descended upon Bronzer and his cronies. The criminals, younger and stronger, fought back. But for each blow they could deliver, they endured several substantial whacks. One by one, the thugs were subdued.

Except for Bronzer. Amidst the fray, Jake saw him flee toward the lobby. *He's going for the guns.* "Julie!" he called, and she joined him as he gave chase.

* * *

Bronzer was hunched over the washing machine trying to pry the door open. Jake glanced at his watch and saw only fifteen seconds left on the locking mechanism timer. "There!" He pointed to the string of holiday lights on the table.

At full speed, he bent low and snatched one of the paint cans collecting the water that leaked from the skylights. He swung his arm around, flinging the can toward Bronzer, striking him in the stomach and causing him to fall.

Julie twirled her arm, creating a snake in the air with the string of lights. She expertly looped layer after layer of lights around Bronzer's shoulders and arms, pinning them close to his torso.

A sudden silence engulfed the lobby. Bronzer cursed and fought, but the strings held firm. Jake stole a look at Julie, whose face was mixed with pride and fear.

"Nice going, Jules," Jake said.

"Oh, no," Julie sighed.

As Bronzer twisted his body around, he wriggled out of his holiday bindings and reached into the washing machine to retrieve his pistol. "I should have dropped you in Lake Michigan when I had the chance."

Jake and Julie instinctively put their hands up and stepped backward.

Dah-dah-dah da ta-da da ta-da. The "Imperial March" ring tone sang from Jake's backpack lying on the ground.

"What's that?" Bronzer yelled.

Jake's eyes lit up: "Discipline."

With large graceful steps, the Dean glided through the broken front door and smashed Bronzer on the base of his skull with his umbrella, sending him unconscious to the ground.

The Dean dusted some snow off his black overcoat and looked at Jake. "I can't even begin to calculate how many demerits this is."

"I'll take them all," Jake panted.

"Hannah called and left a voicemail that you needed help. I would have been here sooner, but I just picked up her message—and of course, the weather slowed me down. I'd called Hannah earlier in the evening, but when she said you weren't here, I spent the evening on the phone trying to figure out what had happened to you."

"Watch out!" Jake hauled Dean Stanley out of the way with one hand and reached for the menorah resting on the nearby hot chocolate table with the other. Bronzer was rising to his feet, his gun still firmly in his hand.

Jake chucked the menorah toward the leaky skylight. The tallest and thickest metal branch of the heavy candelabra struck the glass first, shattering it. With a whumping sound, pounds and pounds of heavy wet snow plunged through the ceiling and buried Bronzer.

"Quick thinking, Jake," the Dean said.

Jake turned toward the hallway as he heard the tell-tale clomps of Ben's feet. Moments later, Ben and Natalie appeared in the lobby, joining Jake and Julie.

"Dean Stanley?" Ben stopped suddenly.

"He just saved us from Bronzer." Jake pointed to the legs sticking out from the pile of snow.

"Cool," Ben replied.

"What's the status?" Jake asked.

"The vets have the rest of them all tied up and are singing their different service songs as they march around in a mini-parade," Natalie said.

Jake started laughing, the massive stress releasing with each breath. *The sergeant major must be loving this.*

With the situation well under control, many residents began to emerge from their rooms. Hannah arrived in the lobby at the same time that the police and the paramedics started flowing through the door. They quickly took charge of the scene, apologizing for the delay in response forced by the storm.

"You and Hannah are close?" Jake asked the Dean.

He nodded. "My older sister lived here for several years before she passed. Hannah took extra-good care of her, right up till the end. We've been dear friends ever since."

*   *   *

"Those guys killed my mom," Jake said quietly.

"I know, Jake. I'm so very sorry." The Dean placed his hand on Jake's shoulder. Together they watched the police cart away the bruised and battered thugs.

Pride, sorrow, relief, happiness—a mix of emotions swirled inside Jake.

We did it, Mom.

Epilogue

While most kids were enjoying spring break, Jake sat in a Chicago courtroom to await the jury's verdict. Assembled together and holding hands, Jake, Ben, Natalie, and Julie were joined by Jake's dad and the other parents, and by Dean Stanley, Maestro Mancini, and Hannah. Annica, Bronzer, and the other criminals stood as they heard the jury foreman read the guilty verdict on every count, including murder, fraud, and kidnapping.

Annica's involvement came as a shock to Chicago's art community. The Hiram Sibley warehouse, which had been passed down from her grandparents, gave her and her cousin, Bronzer, a credible place to "find" the Cassatt. As an intern at the Art Institute, she easily falsified the Watson and Little report.

Having accompanied Karen McGreevy through the authentication process, Annica was able to lie to the museum committee about Karen's thoughts, never mentioning Karen's concern about the eyes. Annica had never intended for anyone to die. But Bronzer killed Rupert Jamison, the National Gallery expert, when he learned from Annica that Rupert had nagging concerns about the painting's style and was planning to amend his report. When Karen started putting those same pieces together, mentioning to Annica that the eyes in the mural differed from those in Cassatt's other works, a nervous Annica alerted Bronzer, who ran Karen down outside the

Chicago Theatre. Jake's arrival, and his crime-solving reputation, signaled another threat, one that Bronzer was determined to thwart.

Jake was happy to reunite with Hannah and the rest of his new Chicago friends. The week following that stormy winter evening had been such a blur. The remaining concerts had been sell-outs and raised a significant amount of money for music programs around the country.

Julie, with newfound confidence in her ribbon exercise, had worked with Samantha and the other girls to help the team improve and ultimately excel.

Ben had played first chair and tackled more solos with ease. He and Natalie were inseparable now, and she was a great steadying influence as he dealt with the reality of his parents' divorce. Natalie vowed to take up rock climbing and conquer her fear of heights. And while Ben lost the computer game competition, he didn't mind, as Natalie had a terrific game room of her own, which she was more than happy to share with him.

The publicity surrounding the capture of the felons at the retirement home attracted a small investor who decided to help the weavers' knitting business get off the ground. The capital raised by the residents was set aside for improvements to the building. First up: a new skylight—and a new menorah.

The sergeant major framed his Leatherman PST, along with a picture of the veterans lined up with the captured men, and presented it to Jake. Jake hung it with pride in his bedroom.

Talking with the Dean, Jake learned the underlying reasons for his unwavering stance on discipline. As he and his friends suspected, the disappearance of Kenneth Matthews crushed the Dean. He invested a great deal of his own money in the security improvements, vowing that harm would never come to another of his students. He had only allowed

Jake and his friends to visit the retirement home because he trusted Hannah to keep an eye on them. Although initially displeased to learn about the excursions the kids took when they were supposed to be at the home, the Dean was unable to stay angry for long. The scar he carried over losing Kenneth, coupled with the constant strain of not knowing what had happened to him, made the Dean empathize with Jake's desire to find out what had happened to his mother.

Jake and his father were present when a crew from the Art Institute carefully dismantled the walls in the Walnut Room. They hugged and openly wept at the sight of the real painting. Jake had accomplished his mother's dream for her—and had captured her killers in the process.

Astonishingly, when they removed the wall covering, the staff discovered a note written in Bertha's hand attached to the back. It read, "This Mary Cassatt mural shall now grace the walls of our dearest friend's fine establishment for the cultural pleasure of all Chicagoans." Clearly, Bertha had not approved its being covered up by walnut.

Renewed interest in the history behind the mural spurred researchers to discover additional details surrounding the placement and subsequent disappearance of the mural. Bertha and Marshall Field had agreed upon the Cassatt's location in the Women's Tea Room, but after Marshall Field died, a new manager of the store wanted a more traditional wood covering. As no other suitable location had been found prior to the mural's being hung in Marshall Field's—and because Mrs. Palmer was out of the country—the store's owners determined that the Cassatt would be safe mounted behind the walnut.

Stored in a temperature-controlled room and protected from light, the mural was in wonderful shape. It didn't take long to restore it—including the piece cut by Jake—to its original splendor. Private donations flooded the Art Institute, all with the request to hang the mural in a new room adjoining the Palmer Gallery. It would be called Karen McGreevy Hall.

When it was time to go home, Jake was sad to say goodbye to Hannah and the others. Never had he imagined he could connect so easily with people five times his age.

Jake and Julie returned home and remained as close as ever. Jake had no idea where their relationship would lead, but for now, that was fine with him—and with Julie. They were just happy to be together. With Jake, Julie knew life would always be an adventure. And with Julie, Jake felt that wherever he was in the world, he was home.

Inspired by the story Maestro Mancini had shared with Jake, which Jake himself shared during an interview, the Art Institute set up a web page dedicated to Karen McGreevy. Within days, hundreds of posts from her school classmates, colleagues, and distant relatives poured in. Jake spent each night reviewing the posts with his father and talking about his mother. One entry included a twenty-minute video that Mr. McGreevy had thought to be lost. It was a news story about Karen and her career. Hearing his mother's voice and watching her on the screen, Jake could see some of the same mannerisms and speech patterns that he knew he exhibited. There was a familiar spark there, too. They were definitely mother and son.

And like the eternal relationship between Lake Michigan and the magnificent city draped along its shore, it was a bond that would last forever.

Chicago Bound is a work of fiction. While the Mary Cassatt mural is real—in the novel, it hangs in the Art Institute of Chicago—in actuality, it disappeared sometime after November 1912, nineteen years after the World's Fair closed, and it has not been seen since. If you have any ideas regarding where the mural might be located, please contact the author at www.seanvogel.com.

Author's Acknowledgements

Creating a book takes time and a team of dedicated professionals. I would like to thank my amazing editors at MB Publishing—Emma Walton Hamilton (our substantive editor), Anne Himmelfarb (our copy editor), and Margie Blumberg (the publisher)—for their devotion, creativity, and enthusiasm. Much gratitude to members of the PageWave Graphics team for their attention to the myriad design details found within these pages. Their artistry can be enjoyed throughout this book. Many thanks to J Loren Reedy, the painter whose beautiful artwork is featured on the cover, as well as on the opening and closing pages. Finally, to Chicago, the Art Institute of Chicago, Mary Cassatt, and the World's Fair of 1893 and all the people who made it a success: inspiration is everything.

The Palace of Fine Arts, now the home of
the Museum of Science and Industry

Mary Cassatt's mural, *Modern Woman*

Left panel

Center panel

Right panel

About the Author

Growing up in a small town in Michigan during the 1980s, Sean Vogel was provided with an excellent garden for cultivating his writing career. With only a few simplistic video games and three television channels, he became an accomplished daydreamer and a creative outside explorer. A son of a garbage truck driver, Sean often received gently used items from his father's route. With a bit of imagination and a little tinkering, these items were reborn as tools for battles against backyard bandits. These childhood adventures, combined with extensive travel experience gained while serving in the U.S. Army, became the inspiration for Jake McGreevy's interest in gadgets and quests for excitement. When Sean's not helping Jake get out of tangles, he is a department manager for a large aerospace company. He lives in Denver with his wife and daughter and their two dachshunds.

Made in the USA
Charleston, SC
26 October 2013